WEEPING ANGELS

HEATHER D VEINOTTE

Heather Veinotte

COPYRIGHT

person, please purchase an additional copy for each recipient. If you're reading this book and did not purchase it, or it was not purchased for your use only, then please return to your favorite e-book retailer and purchase your own copy. Thank you for respecting the hard work of this author.

ISBN ebook 978-0-9734559-8-4

ISBN Print978-0-9734559-7-7

DEDICATION

This book is dedicated to my husband Bruce who will always be the wind beneath my wings.

PROLOGUE

Lunenburg, Nova Scotia, 1895

Emma Ramey stood in the bay window of their Lunenburg home and watched her father's ships sail past the Battery in Lunenburg Harbor. Tears ran down her face when the first ship, with its three sails billowing in the wind, raised and lowered its flag three times. Out of habit, Emma forced a smile and waved though she knew her husband John couldn't see her.

Her unborn child kicked. She stroked her stomach and chuckled. "You're the reason I'm standing here, instead of on the deck of your papa's ship."

Startled by the sound of laughter behind her, Emma spun around. She smiled at her twin sister Olive, who stood near the top of the kitchen stairs.

Emma sighed. "Oh Ollie, did you see them wave as they passed the Battery?"

Olive ran up the rest of the stairs, even though she was with child and joined her sister in front of the bay window. The identical young women, almost a month short of twenty-two, wrapped their arms around each other's waists and watched the ships, carrying the men they loved, disappear around Kaulback's Point.

Olive looked down at her stomach and sighed. "I pleaded with Elbert to let me go with him. But Papa and our husbands decided it was safer for us to stay in Lunenburg and look after each other." She put her hands on her hips. "Without consulting us."

Emma swiped at her wet cheeks and hugged her sister. "They'll be back in a few months. Just in time for your baby to arrive."

"Papa could be a grandfather when he returns." Olive laughed and touched Emma's little bump on her stomach. "And if they're late, we might be celebrating two births when they return."

Emma squeezed her sister's arm. "And I'm betting there'll be lots of wonderful things brought back for our new babies on those ships, if I know our men folk."

"Beggin' your pardon, Miss." Katie, Emma's maid, moved to stand behind them as she entered the kitchen from the back stairs. Katie was sixteen and straight from Ireland. She had thick curly auburn hair and green eyes that twinkled with good humor.

Katie curtsied. "Your tea is ready and Cook wants to know where you'll be havin' it?"

Emma smiled at the younger girl. "Thanks Katie, we'll come to the kitchen and eat with you and Cook."

Olive sniffed the air. "*Mm-mm*, is that gingerbread?"

Katie grinned and curtsied. "That it is, ma'am. Hot out of the oven."

"Now Katie, haven't I told you that you don't need to curtsey when you speak to us." Emma crossed her arms on her chest and pretended to scold Katie.

"That you have, Ma'am."

She curtsied again and giggled, skipping lightly down the stairs to the kitchen.

The sisters took one last look at the harbor and had turned to go for tea when Katie's screams ripped through the air.

Olive grabbed Emma. "What in God's name is happening?"

Olive pulled the hem of her skirt up to her thigh with one hand and grabbing the bannister for support with her free hand, ran down the stairs as fast as she could. Emma, terrified for her sister, followed close behind her. "Oh Ollie, be careful."

Both women rushed through the wide-open kitchen door at the same time. Ollie's screams filled the air and Emma grabbed the door frame for support.

The kitchen floor flowed red. Cook lay face down by the open oven door in a pool of her own blood. Sweet Katie, giggling just minutes earlier, lay sprawled across the long kitchen table, amid chards of broken china. Her once-beautiful, green, laughing eyes...vacant. Horror and shock etched her face. Steaming clumps of gingerbread lay scattered everywhere, the strong aroma of ginger smell mixing with the metallic smell of blood.

Olive and Emma screamed. Emma swallowed the bile that rose in her throat. The twins stood rooted to the spot, not knowing what to do. Fighting the urge to faint, Emma sobbed. "Oh my God. Betty...Katie."

Bang! The kitchen door slammed shut behind them with such force that the cups in the hutch rattled. The girls screamed and turned toward the door.

Reeking of cheap whiskey, Ian McGregor stood there, barring the only way out with his huge body. He clutched a butcher's knife, still dripping blood. His hate-filled eyes stared at the terrified girls that stood close to him, clutching each other. The stench of cheap whiskey from his filthy body was so strong it almost masked the scent of death that oozed from every corner of the kitchen.

Blood trickled down his beard from long deep scratches on his face. McGregor staggered toward them, the bloody knife held high over his shoulder. Gloating, he fed on the terror that covered their faces. Throwing his head back, he roared with satanic laughter, sending shivers of dread through them.

He stood in front of them and wiped the blood from the deep scratches on his face. He pointed the knife at Katie's body. "See what happened to that little bitch when she scratched me?" He spit at Olive, the bloody mucus hitting her face.

He roared again with laughter when she cringed. "Now I got Archie Ramey's spoiled little brats right where I want 'em."

Olive hung on to Emma, whimpering with fear. "Mr. McGregor? Why are you doing this? Why?" With the last word, she moaned and fainted. Emma screamed as she caught her sister. Olive was dead weight in her arms. She backed away from the monster and gently laid the unconscious Olive on the floor.

She glared at him. "You beast. You filthy, rotten beast."

He moved closer to her. "You ain't seen nothin' yet, miss high and mighty. Just like your old man, ain't ya? You and your sister here, struttin' around Lunenburg like ya own the place."

He lurched toward Emma. She backed away from him, ever closer to the kitchen wall by the stove. In that moment she knew there was no escape. The back door was too far away.

McGregor stopped and pulled a bottle from a torn pocket of his filthy jacket. He ripped out the cork with blackened, decayed teeth. Then he spit it out. Emma watched the cork fly through the air, land and bounce on little Katie's lifeless body. Tilting the bottle to his lips, he guzzled. Streams of whiskey, escaping the corners of his mouth seeped into his dirt-encrusted beard.

He wiped his mouth with the back of his hand and smashed the bottle against the wall. When he bellowed with more horrible laughter it almost froze the blood in Emma's veins. She watched in terror as Satan personified, staggered closer.

"Please. Please don't do this. Please," Emma cried, her hands outstretched, begging for their lives.

He hacked deep in his throat and spit at Emma, hitting the bodice of her dress.

"An eye for an eye. Ain't that what the bible reads? He fired me and hid my woman and my brat away from me. No man ain't tellin' me, I can't beat my woman. She belongs to me."

He leered at Emma. "Just like Archie Ramey's brats belong to him."

McGregor stepped over Olive's motionless body. He stopped and stared down at her lying on the floor. Slowly, he raised his head and smiled at Emma, a smile that came straight from hell. He kept smiling at her, as he thrust his knife deep into Olive's chest.

"You'll regret the day you ever laid eyes on me, Archie Ramey." He swore as he pulled the knife out and once again plunged it into Olive's motionless body.

Emma screamed and screamed, as her heart tore to pieces. "No Ollie. Oh my God, Ollie, no. Ollie."

Without missing a beat, he pulled out the blood-covered knife from Olive's chest and moved toward her.

Emma couldn't stop screaming. Her throat was raw. Hope dwindling with every step he took toward her. It was unlikely someone, anyone would come to help before it was too late.

He closed in.

Emma shielded her stomach with her arms and desperately said the Lord's Prayer.

Crazed, he moved in. "The Lord ain't gonna help ya, Missy. The Lord be damned. You're all mine."

She tried backing away from the monster in front of her, but she was trapped. The coat hooks on the kitchen wall dug painfully into her back. She sobbed uncontrollably for her Ollie, who lay in a pool of blood by her feet.

He stopped, towering over her. She gagged and retched as his putrid breath seeped into every pore of her body. Emma lashed out, pounding the monster with both fists, but the animal reared back and laughed at her feeble attempt to survive.

He grabbed Emma up with one filthy, bear-paw-sized hand, lifting her right off the floor.

She fought with all the strength she had, while searching for any way to escape. "Please, please." Her voice was only a whisper. "I beg of you. Please."

More manic laughter echoed through the room as he threw Emma to the floor. His eyes never left her face as he slowly raised the knife – still dripping with Olive's blood – into the air above his shoulder.

She screamed and screamed as agonizing waves of pain ripped through her body. Darkness encircled her and with her last breath, Emma sobbed for the child she would never hold in her arms.

1

"Welcome to Nova Scotia in the summer." Melissa Gordon talked to herself as she strained to see the road through the water-drenched windshield of her rental Jeep. The theme from *Ghostbusters* suddenly filled the SUV's interior. She chuckled at the choice of music her cousin Kelsey had put on her phone.

She tapped her blue tooth. "Hello, you're speaking to Mel Gordon."

"Hi, Dear."

"Aunt Jo. It's great to hear from you."

"Where are you, Mel?"

Melissa Gordon, known to everyone as Mel, peered through the windshield and sighed. "I'm not sure. Somewhere between Halifax and Lunenburg. My GPS says that I have to travel fifteen more miles before I reach the Lunenburg ramp."

"Mel, dear, what on earth is that noise?"

Mel chuckled. "That, my dear aunt, is the rain pounding on the roof of my Jeep."

"Good grief, that sounds dangerous. Should you be driving?"

"Well I can't see to stop, so I may as well keep going." She swore as the SUV hydroplaned on the water-covered highway. Carefully, she pulled the Jeep back to the correct side of the watery road.

"Mel? What's wrong?"

"It's okay. I just hydroplaned a bit and it scared me. I'll tell you what, Aunt Jo, I'll call you as soon as I get to Lunenburg. Okay?"

There was a pause from the other end. "Okay, dear. I just wanted to check and see how you were doing."

Probably because of David. Mel felt her eyes well up and swiped at a tear that trickled down her cheek. Just the thought of David still made her weepy.

Mel sighed. "I know why you called, Aunt Jo. This was supposed to be my wedding day."

"Yes, it was, and that bastard was sick enough to pick this day for *his* wedding day."

This made Mel smile in spite of herself. Aunt Jo wouldn't say bat guano with her mouth full, so Mel knew how upset her aunt was.

Mel peered through the windshield. "I'm just glad I found out before we were married."

A sigh caught on a sob in her throat and she took a deep breath before she continued. "I must be unique. It's not every day that the groom leaves his bride for one of her bridesmaids."

"Unique or not, I can't understand why he had to announce it at a dinner party with all your friends present."

Mel wiped another tear from her cheek. "Okay. Enough about David. I think the rain is letting up." She looked at the GPS. "I'm almost ten miles from the Lunenburg exit. I'll call you when I get settled."

There was silence on the other end. She knew that Aunt Jo was weighing whether to say more, or not.

"Please don't worry about me, Aunt Jo. I'm a big girl. I'm a ghostbuster, remember?"

Aunt Jo sighed from thousands of miles away. "Yes, you are, and one of the best ones I've ever worked with, but you're still my baby and this day must bring back difficult memories and lots of what ifs."

Mel gritted her teeth. She had to get Aunt Jo off this subject or else she'd start bawling like a baby.

"The rain is letting up, Aunt Jo."

She checked the GPS.

"I'm getting closer to the Lunenburg exit and have to focus. I'll call you as soon as I'm settled. I promise."

There was more silence before her aunt sighed. "Alright Mel, but if you want me to come and take over, do not hesitate to call. You need to get away and forget what the jerk did to you. I can be there in no time. I really think you should pass on this job."

Mel breathed deeply. "You don't understand, Aunt Jo. I need to do this. It's better for me to keep busy this way. I'm here to get rid of a pesky ghost. That will take my mind off the asshole."

Her aunt's silence on the other end of the phone spoke volumes about her concern.

Mel sighed. "I promise you – If I change my mind, I'll call you right away."

"Okay, honey. I'll hold you to that promise. Love you."

Mel smiled at their life-long salutation. "Love you too, Aunt Jo. Give Uncle Andrew a hug for me."

They disconnected and Mel gripped the steering wheel so hard, her knuckles hurt, as she remembered her last conversation with David. He'd called her and her family "freaks of nature." Shouting hateful words that ripped through her heart like a knife. He'd laughed at her tears as he told her he'd never loved her that not even the Gordon money could make him accept what her family stood for... That he couldn't wait to be rid of her – so he could declare to the world that Liz was the love of his life.

So, Liz and David had taken over her wedding venue and invited all their friends and relatives.

She saluted the happy couple with her middle finger.

"To both of you."

She sighed when her phone rang again. She didn't want to re-hash her canceled wedding with Aunt Jo right now, or anyone else for that matter.

She answered resignedly. "Mel Gordon speaking." No response, yet she knew she had made a connection because she heard background noise.

She tried again. "Mel Gordon speaking. Hello."

"I apologize Ms. Gordon. This is Edward White speaking. I thought you'd be a man and your voice caught me off guard."

Mel chuckled. "Mel is short for Melissa. Is that a problem, Mr. White?"

"No, not at all. I was just surprised, that's all, Ms. Gordon."

Mel chuckled. "Don't worry. You're not the first and probably won't be the last. And please, call me Mel."

"Alright, Mel, I just called to see where you were and how you're doing in this storm."

She smiled. "That's so kind of you. I'm approaching the Lunenburg exit."

"That's great, I'll meet you at the Mourning Rose, a B&B in the heart of Lunenburg. I'm staying there as well. You have the coordinates?"

"I do and I'm driving a black Jeep. See you there." She ended the call and drove onto the exit ramp.

The rain stopped as she drove through the picturesque town of Mahone Bay. Mel spoke out loud. "Wow, what a beautiful town." She and her family all had the same trait of speaking their thoughts. Her family thought it was normal to talk to themselves, but as far as David was concerned, he'd seen nothing normal about the Gordon family.

Her Aunt Jo and Uncle Andrew owned and ran the Gordon Agency, a unique business wherein all the employees had special gifts – or curses, depending on who you spoke to. Some were mediums or psychics. The strongest gifts ran down through the generations of Scottish women in the Gordon family.

The men usually were "sensitive," but their gifts weren't as strong as their sisters', mothers', etc. The Gordon Agency was well known and often called upon when no one else could help. Some were psychics or mediums. Others like Mel and Aunt Jo were ghostbusters, with a few other talents thrown in to make things interesting. Her cousin, Kelsey, could do all of the above as had Mel's dead mother and aunt.

When Mel and her cousin Kelsey were just toddlers, both sets of parents died in a skiing accident. Their Aunt Jo and Uncle Andrew adopted the girls and helped them handle the special gifts that had been bequeathed to them from their ancestors.

Mel drove past Lunenburg's welcome sign just inside the town limits and gasped. It was as if she had turned back the pages of time to the nineteenth century. Stately homes edged the sidewalks and these majestic wooden matrons still held their own from a bygone era, proudly displaying wraparound verandas and stained-glass windows that welcomed Mel into their midst.

Beep-beep-beep. Startled by the noise, Mel glanced at the GPS. An annoying voice stated that her arrival had taken one hour from the airport. The stress-filled drive in the pouring rain had seemed more like three hours and the little chat with Aunt Jo about her canceled wedding day to David, the jerk, hadn't helped shorten it a bit.

She eased into a parking place almost in front of the entrance of a grand Victorian mansion with double bay windows upstairs and down. She jumped out of the Jeep and stretched out the tension.

Mel turned and faced the B&B just as a tall, smiling man came down the steps toward her. She didn't have to have special gifts to know that this was Edward White, her new boss – and wow, what a handsome boss he was. She smiled at the cliché, tall dark and handsome, but the description fit Edward White to perfection: tall and muscular – around six feet – with distinguished hints of silver tipping the sides of his temples and lightly frosting his dark hair. Edward was a producer in the film industry, and he could easily be a leading man in any movie.

As he moved closer, she guessed he was about ten years older than her thirty-four years and wished – just for a moment – she had her cousin, Kelsey's gift to read minds.

He smiled at her as he joined her by the Jeep.

"Mel?"

She smiled and he took her hand in his. "I'm Edward White."

"Thanks for meeting me, Mr. White."

He smiled. "Please, call me Edward."

Shaking her hand, he smiled and added, "I'll help you with your luggage."

She opened the back of the jeep and pulled out one suit-case and a soft canvas bag.

He stared at the back of the empty Jeep. "Wow, you really travel light for a, um, ghostbuster."

She grinned. "I left my proton pack at home."

He gawked at her. "You're kidding, right?"

She laughed, grabbed her tool bag and passed it to Edward.

"Of course, I'm kidding." She held up the canvas bag to him. "This, is how I travel."

By the time she'd carried her suitcase from the jeep to the outside steps of the B&B, her muscles were aching. The suitcase was heavy and she wished she had given it to Edward instead of her bag.

Mel planted a fixed smile on her face. She silently groaned as she dragged her suitcase up the twelve brick steps to the front entrance. "Wow, what a lot of steps in this place."

He turned and nodded his head. No way was this handsome hunk going to hear her grunt or groan trying to lift the suitcase. *What in heaven's name did I pack?*

She smiled her thanks at Edward as he held the open door for her to pass. Mel stopped short. She couldn't believe her eyes. Between her and the reception desk, which she planned to collapse on, were another six steep steps.

Edward smiled at her. "I love the architecture in Lunenburg. This originally belonged to a sea captain who spent a lot of time in Europe."

Mel struggled up the final set of steps with her suitcase, mumbling under her breath. "I'm betting it was countries with a lot of steps."

Finally, she could use the wheels. So, she tugged on the handle, pulling her suitcase up the last step then followed Edward to the receptionist who stood behind a waist-high, oak counter at the foot of a wide staircase.

Edward leaned over the counter. "Miss Mel Gordon is checking in."

A pretty young girl in her twenties wore a nametag that read: Louise. She smiled, but looked puzzled. "I have a Mr. Mel Gordon registered... No Ms. Gordon."

Mel cut in. "That's me. I'm Mel Gordon."

Louise smiled. "Oh, sorry, Ms. Gordon. Welcome to the Mourning Rose. We hope you enjoy your stay and if there's anything you need, please don't hesitate to call the front desk."

Mel smiled at her. "Thank you, Louise."

She looked around the main lobby. "What a beautiful old building."

Edward nodded and turned back to Louise and asked about a package delivery he was expecting.

Mel stood, leaned against the desk and watched as a young couple, dressed in turn of the century costume, walked arm in arm across the lobby.

The woman smiled at her and the man tipped his finger to his forehead in salutation. They walked past the reception desk toward the large arched opening of the dining room.

The woman, in her early twenties, smiled adoringly at the man as he murmured something in her ear. A soft musical laugh filled Mel's head as the lady in taffeta tapped her escort on the arm with her fan. Mel smiled at them and nodded back as they faded away in front of her.

She smiled and murmured. "My goodness, the spirit world is alive and well in this bed and breakfast."

Edward turned and took her bag from her hand. "There, I checked in for you." She reached for her purse and he shook his head.

"No. All expenses are covered on this job."

Mel smiled sheepishly. "I really didn't go over the contract before I left the office."

Edward handed her a key. "You have a suite on the third floor."

"A suite?"

He nodded. "Did you notice the two large bay windows on the top of the house when you entered?"

"Yes, they're stunning."

"The left window or 'bump,' as it's known in Lunenburg, is your suite and the right one is mine. We're across the hall from each other."

He looked at her. "I hope you're comfortable with that."

Mel laughed. "That's fine. Remind me to tell you about some of the places I've had to sleep. I can assure you, most of my sleeping quarters didn't have any sitting room to relax in."

Edward smiled. "I'll take you up on that, soon. Well then, let's get you settled. Driving in the storm from the airport had to be an exhausting trip. I've done it enough times in the rain myself."

Before she and Edward moved to the elegant staircase, she leaned over the desk and spoke to Louise.

"Louise, do you think the Mourning Rose is haunted?"

Louise nodded and leaned closer. "Sometimes, the staff hear things. Footsteps coming down the stairs. Even laughter and then when they try to find out where it's coming from, it just stops. It's so weird."

Mel smiled at the young woman. "Do you ever hear something like taffeta rustling?"

Louise's eyes widened with surprise. "How did you know that?"

Mel smiled at the young girl's confusion. "Oh, just a wild guess."

Edward, took her suitcase and opened a narrow door between the desk and the staircase. It appeared to be a small closet. He placed all of Mel's luggage inside the small room and closed the door. Louise moved from behind the desk.

Edward put his hand up. "It's fine Louise, I'll bring them up."

Mel quizzed Edward. "Bring them up? But you just put my bags in there."

"This is a lift for luggage that was installed almost a hundred and fifty years ago."

Nodding, Louise chimed in. "And it still works. It really saves us a lot of heavy lugging up and down three flights of stairs." She smiled at Mel. "I hope you have a wonderful and uneventful stay."

Mel followed Edward as he climbed to the third floor. The steps were still wide, but not as grand as the first two stories of the B&B.

Mel didn't mind following Edward up the stairs. He had a great body and his jeans fit to perfection. *Nice butt, Mr. White.* She smiled to herself.

At the third floor, she made a vow to renew her gym pass as soon as she returned home. She mumbled a special thanks to the inventor of the lift because without it she would have collapsed on the top of her suitcase by the beginning of the second level.

Edward walked to a narrow door close to the head of the stairs. He opened it and pulled the ropes hanging beside the door. In no time at all, her luggage arrived and sat in front of them.

"Oh my gosh, that's ingenious."

He passed Mel her suitcase. "There you go. At least now you don't have to carry this up any more steps."

His eyes twinkled at her.

Mel felt herself blush. "You noticed, huh?"

He chuckled. "It was pretty hard not to, with all the puffing and grunting you were doing just to get your suitcase to the desk in the lobby."

She took her suitcase and pulled the handle from the body of the case. "Well, hats off to the guy who invented this lift."

Edward nodded. "It's amazing how practical and inventive our forefathers were."

He unlocked the door to Mel's room and she followed him into a charming sitting room.

"Oh my, isn't this lovely. My Aunt Jo loves antiques. She'd love this place."

Cream Victorian loveseats, with rounded occasional chairs, picked up the soothing colors of the green and cream wall paper, filling the sitting room with a sense of serenity. In the bedroom, a four-poster bed, filled with throw cushions of every description, welcomed an afternoon of reading or napping. A lovely antique desk sat by the window, just the right size for her laptop. Across from the desk, Mel opened a door to the bathroom. A huge, old-fashioned claw foot tub dwarfed the room. An ornate shelf beside the tub overflowed with candles, soft towels and pretty bottles filled with bath crystals. All just waiting to be used for a long luxurious soak.

Mel clapped her hands and smiled at Edward. "I can hardly wait to try this beauty out."

Edward, following behind her, looked around. "This suite is very nice. It's even nicer than mine."

She grinned. "Would you like to trade?"

He looked at her, not sure if she was joking.

What a serious, but kind man, she thought.

Mel moved to the large curved window and looked out over the panoramic view of Lunenburg and its harbor. Beautiful old Victorian homes elbowed each other along both sides of the street – reminding her of old dowagers fighting for their place of prominence in bygone Lunenburg society.

"Oh, my. This is breathtaking."

Edward came and stood beside her, taking in the view. "It is, isn't it? I never grow tired of it. Enjoy. We have the same window and the same view. We're standing in what is referred around here as a Lunenburg Bump."

Mel quizzed him. "Bump?"

Edward nodded and grinned. "Bump."

Mel smiled. "What a fun name for a beautiful architectural design."

"Enjoy the view. I'm going next door to make a few phone calls. I'll come back for you in a bit and we'll go for dinner. I'll call you first to see if you're ready before I come and get you."

Mel nodded absently to Edward as he left her room. She stood in front of her window and watched a woman in period dress walking back and forth in front of the Mourning Rose, wringing her hands.

"Oh dear," Mel murmured. "Wringing... She's wringing her hands. That can't be good."

She crossed the hall and knocked on Edward's door. He opened it, his cell at his ear.

"Edward, sorry to bother you. Is there some kind of celebration in Lunenburg this week?"

"Celebration?"

"Yes, you know, old home week or something, where everyone dresses in period costumes."

Edward looked puzzled. "No, I don't think so."

Mel sighed. "Okay, that's what I thought."

He quirked his eyebrow. "Why do you ask?"

"No reason. I'll be right back. Edward."

"Where are you going?"

"Just outside."

She ran down two flights of stairs but slowed when she reached the main staircase, so Louise would see she had a few manners.

When she reached the sidewalk, the anxious woman was still there, pacing back and forth in front of the B&B.

Mel sat on the low wall that separated the postage stamp-sized lawn of the Mourning Rose from the sidewalk.

The woman passed her a few times before Mel put out her hand and telepathically spoke to her.

"Hello, Ma'am. Do you need some help?"

Two girls, giggling over something on a smartphone,

walked past Mel and through the woman that had stopped to look at her.

The specter stared frantically at Mel.

Her voice was clear in Mel's mind. "*I don't know. I don't know what to do.*" She wrung her hands. "*I can't find my little girlie. She was here just a bit ago and now she's gone. Did you see her?*"

Mel patted the wall where she sat. The woman sat down beside her, tears running down her transparent cheeks.

"*I'm Melissa.*"

"*My name is Flossie Sarty. I have to find my Edith. She's just a little thing and she's scared of the horses. She's so frightened of them.*"

Mentally, Mel spoke to Flossie in a very slow and soft voice. "*Flossie, I know where Edith is.*"

Tears filled the specter's eyes and she wrung her hands in anguish. "*You know where my little girlie is?*"

Mel nodded her head. "*She's safe Flossie and she's waiting for you.*"

"*Oh, thank goodness. My poor baby. She'll be so scared without me. I need to go to her.*"

Mel nodded. "*Yes, you do. You've been apart too long.*"

Flossie's words tore at the strings of Mel's heart as the woman sobbed. "*She's all I have left. Where's my little girlie? She needs me so bad. Is she hurtin' for me?*"

"*She's very close to you. I can take you to her, but you must do everything I say. Okay?*"

More transparent tears ran down the dead woman's cheeks. "*Yes. Yes, please. I'll do anything to find my baby. She has to be so scared without me. She's all I have left.*"

Mel took a deep breath and let it out. "*Flossie, try to stay calm and close your eyes.*"

"*But, I don't want to close my eyes. I want to look for my Edith.*"

Mel kept her voice as calm and soothing as she could. It

was obvious this poor specter had been hurting and confused for such a long time.

"You need to be calm for Edith because she's been looking for you too, remember? So, close your eyes Flossie, focus on the light that's above you. Do you see the light?"

Flossie nodded her head and clasped her hands together at her breast. *"There it is. I see it. It's comin' round me. Is my baby there?"*

"She is. She's been waiting a long time for you. You're doing great, Flossie. Let that light surround you. Do you feel it surrounding you?"

"I do. Oh my. It's so beautiful."

Mel took a deep breath. *"Flossie, look into the very center of the light."*

Flossie sobbed. *"Oh Edith. I see my baby. My sweet girlie."*

Mel sighed. *"Go home to her, Flossie. She's been waiting a long time."*

Flossie sobbed with joy. *"Oh, my little girlie, I'm comin'. Mamma's comin'."*

Mel sat and watched as Flossie faded completely from the sidewalk wall.

Expelling a deep breath, Mel clung to the cement wall with both hands as she inhaled as much oxygen as she could. When her breathing had returned to normal, she mumbled under her breath.

"Wow. This one took a lot of energy." Mel had felt her energy drain slowly from her as she'd tried to help Flossie and it was a relief that the crossover had been a success.

Still, Mel grabbed two small packages of brown sugar from the side pocket of her jeans, tore the tops off and shook the contents of both packets into her mouth. Almost immediately she felt the sugar work its magic, bringing energy back into her body.

The sun peeked through rain-drenched clouds yet a shadow blocked it from warming her. She looked up to see

Edward standing over her. Unasked questions quirked his sexy eyebrows.

"Mel, what's going on?" I watched from the window and I saw you talking to yourself. It looked like you were having a conversation with someone I couldn't see."

She nodded, took another packet of brown sugar from her pocket, tore it open, shook it into her mouth and swallowed.

He smiled at her. "Um, do you have a habit I should know about before we proceed further into our business arrangement?"

She smiled back. "No, you're safe. It's just brown sugar. You're right on the mark though. I was speaking to a lovely lady called Flossie and now she's gone to be with her little girl, Edith."

"Edith? Gone where?" He looked around the yard and down the street.

Mel smiled at him. "Yes, Edith. Flossie, and her daughter, would have been about one hundred years old now."

Edward was shocked. "A ghost was here? Right here?" He pointed to the wall where Mel still sat.

Mel smiled. "Yup. Right here." She patted the wall beside her.

She checked her watch. "This has to be a record. I've been here forty-five minutes. Two ghosts smiled at me in the foyer of the B&B and I've just helped a mother cross over to be with her little girl."

"Cross over?"

Mel looked at him and laughed at his confusion. "Oh my, I think I'm going to have to teach you 'Ghostie 101'."

She jumped up from the wall but lost her balance. "Oops. That happens sometimes."

Edward caught her in his arms to steady her. Mel smiled her thanks. *That felt nice.*

Her stomach growled and she shrugged. "That's how it

goes. Now, I'm very hungry. Come and have dinner with me. My treat, and while we eat, you can tell me all about my assignment."

Edward ran his hand through his hair. "Well it's simple. We want you to get rid of a ghost."

"That's why I'm here."

A car pulled up behind her Jeep and a man in his mid-thirties jumped out and ran to where they stood.

Edward waved. "Josh, I'm glad you're here. I want you to meet Mel. Mel this is Josh Wells. One of the best producers in the business."

"Hi, nice to meet you." Josh took her outstretched hand.

"We thought you'd be a man."

Mel stood with her arms extended and grinned at them. "Ta da." They all laughed.

Josh turned to Edward. "I've been trying to reach you. Your phone must be dead."

Edward pulled his phone from his shirt pocket. "Damn. I must have turned it off."

"We have a problem. The large overhead, long-shot camera for the front of the house has been smashed."

Edward swore under his breath. "Smashed? How did that happen?"

Josh shrugged. "The usual way. It lifted off the floor and flew against the wall. I think you'd better come see for yourself. There's not much of it left."

Mel took her keys out of her pocket and waved them in front of the men.

"You lead, Josh, and we'll follow you in my Jeep. I think it's time I met this ghost on its home turf."

She jumped into the Jeep, with Edward taking the passenger side, and followed Josh around one-way streets and up steep hills.

"Wow. Lunenburg is one big hill."

Edward grinned. "It certainly is. The one-way streets take a little getting used to, but look around. No matter where you are in Lunenburg, there's an amazing view of the harbor."

He pointed to the hill across from the town on the other side of the harbor. "The golf course is one of a kind. I've golfed all over the world, but the panoramic view of Lunenburg from the greens is one in a million."

Mel gasped as they turned the corner. "Oh, my gosh. What a gorgeous church."

"It is. That's St. John's Anglican Church, second oldest standing protestant church in North America. There's a lot of filming in Lunenburg because it resembles New England so much."

Edward gestured with his hand. "Turn right. Then left." And they did.

Mel turned into a cul-de-sac and came face to face with an elegant, Italian revival Victorian mansion and parked behind Josh. The beauty of the home took her breath away.

"Here we are."

Wooden shingles, designed as scallop shells, dressed the matron in regal robes. Heavy gingerbread edgings on all corners of the house added whimsical, crowning touches.

"Wow, what a house."

From the sidewalk, they walked up five wide curved steps in burgundy and cream Italian Marble that led to the front entrance. At the bottom of the steps, two Greek-styled, black wrought iron urns overflowed with burgundy rose bushes – sentinels guarding their dowager queen. Two more identical urns flanked the entrance at the top of the steps.

"Oh my gosh, look at that door. It's beautiful, Edward."

At the front entrance, a wide stained-glass door and two side windows were covered with the same flowing scene, depicting three ships, with raised sails, on an ocean of burgundy. On either side of the grand entrance, four two-story stained-glass pavilion windows were shimmering in color as the red washed sky of sunset burst through the few shreds of storm clouds that were left.

"Edward, this is absolutely stunning."

"Yes, it is. Welcome to my hell."

2

When Edward opened the door they almost collided with two men hastily exiting the building. A scream from inside, ripped through the air as they ran down the steps.

The younger man stopped close to Mel, but the older man kept going until he reached the other side of the street.

Josh, followed by Edward, Mel and the man on the steps ran across the street to join the older man who stood there staring at the house.

"Dan, what happened?" Edward asked.

Dan, a tall man in his early fifties, was bent over trying to catch his breath. He stood up and looked sheepishly at Mel when she approached. Then his attention shifted...

"Edward, you've got to do something. We're running out of cameras and nerves."

Edward patted him on the back. "I know, I know. But help has arrived. Dan, this is Mel Gordon."

Dan shook her hand, but also his head. "She's a woman, Edward. No disrespect, Miss Gordon, but you can't handle what's going on inside. "Hell..." He pointed to the younger man standing beside Mel. "Lenny here did two stints in the Gulf and likely can't even get the nerve to go back in."

Edward took a hand and ran it through his hair. "What happened this time?"

Dan shook his head. "Whatever that thing is, it picked Lenny up on the stairs. Man, you should have seen him. He was dangling two feet above the steps. With his legs kicking and he was punching out at something I couldn't see."

"What did you see in the same area when Lenny was hanging in the air? Think very carefully, Dan," Mel said as she tried to calm him, but it was obvious that talking about what he had seen was agitating him.

"Well it got kinda dark at the foot of the stairs and it looked almost like a shadow, but I never thought anything of that because the sun shining through the stained-glass windows creates shadows on the wall. But then the shadow moved across the wall. It had a human shape and headed for Lenny." He paused and shook his head. "I just stood there, stunned. Suddenly Lenny was in the air, shaking back and forth. Then, right in front of my eyes, the shadow threw him down so hard that he rolled down the stairs and the only thing that saved him was that his foot caught between the rungs of the bannister and slowed his fall. I ran up the stairs and grabbed Lenny and we both got the hell out of there." Dan wiped the sweat from his face. "Lenny could have broken his neck, Edward."

Edward ran his hand through his hair again and shook his head, resigned. "I know. I know."

He joined Lenny where he sat on a bench and talked to the man. Lenny nodded. Edward patted his back and then they stood and joined the others.

Edward introduced Mel to Lenny and Dan. "Guys, this is Mel Gordon. She's been hired to help us get rid of whatever is plaguing us. So, we can get back on track before we have to shut down production."

Lenny looked at her and blushed. "I'm sorry ma'am, for seemin' like such a coward, but I ain't had nothin' like that happen before – even in the military."

Mel smiled at him. "Don't worry, Lenny. In my profession, I've learned to do the mile sprint faster than most Olympic runners. Our motto is 'Don't stick around. Run'."

"Excuse me, ma'am. I mean no disrespect, but whatever it is in there, a little biddy thing like you is no match for it. I've seen a lot of things in my years, but I have never had anything that made me run like that. Now I know what a hound dog feels, running for its life with its tail between his legs after he's been beaten by a coon." He lowered his head in embarrassment. "'Tis a sad sight, ma'am," he said, his southern drawl very noticeable. He took his hat off and twisted it around in his hands.

Suddenly, another scream ripped through the air, followed by intense sobbing.

Lenny straightened up. "Lordy, lordy. Did you hear that?"

Dan rolled his eyes. "Sobbing? Man, that's a new one. We haven't heard that before."

Edward looked at Mel. "Well one way or another, we have to get to the bottom of what's causing this. But after what just happened here I can't let you do this. Too dangerous, Mel."

She shook her head. "Now just a moment Edward. Do you think that I can't handle what's going on inside this house? I assure you I can."

Edward shook his head. "No, I think that you might be able to handle it. I just don't want you to get hurt in the process. Look what it did to Lenny here, and he's twice your size."

Mel rolled her eyes at them. "I can honestly say that what

you have experienced here is so far down on my list of incidents that I've had to deal with over the years, that it isn't funny."

The men stared at her with their mouths hanging open.

Edward quirked his eyebrows at her. "Are you serious?"

Mel nodded. "Very much so. Now step aside. I want to see what's going on in there."

She entered the vestibule of the beautiful home and stood listening to the sobbing. Hatred bombarded her senses mixed with over-whelming sadness.

Josh's voice cut into her thoughts. "Cripes look at what it did this time."

They followed her and stood in the foyer taking in the destruction around them.

"Oh, my God, look at this place. This will cost a fortune to replace and repair." Josh wrung his hands. "The crew won't take much more of this, Edward. Some of them are talking about leaving."

Another piercing scream ripped through the air and vibrated inside Mel, reaching the very marrow of her bones.

She gave the men credit for holding their ground. Mel, who had seen all this before, was perturbed.

She turned and faced the men who stood behind her. "How long has this been going on?"

Josh shrugged. "For as long as we've been here."

Manic laughter echoed around them.

Mel put her hands in the air. "And that noise?"

Josh shrugged. "Oh, the laughing? That's just part of the fun of this place. After the screaming, we hear the laughter. It wasn't bad at first but with every passing week it's getting worse. In the beginning, things would just move around." He looked at Edward for confirmation. "And now, furniture's thrown at us and some has been destroyed."

Mel moved further into the large foyer. The men followed

close behind her, as if trying to protect her. "When did it start?" she asked.

Lenny tipped his head to one side, deep in thought. "I'd say that it was after the movie wound up and a little after we started doing runs for the television series. Little things at first, but within a month we were just about where we are now. This last week, the attacks are happening more often. Ma'am, I hate to say this, but it's almost like it's getting stronger by the day. I can tell you, I haven't seen anything like this back in North Carolina and some strange things happen up in the hills."

Mel smiled at Lenny. "I know Lenny, I've been there."

She stood very still and closed her eyes. When she opened them again, she looked at Edward. "I'll need a trip to the hardware store."

Edward looked at her as if she had two heads. "Hardware store?"

Mel nodded and looked at the stunned men staring at her. "I'm going to need a lot more magnets."

Edward stared at her. "Magnets?"

"Yes, that's right, magnets. Edward, I don't know how to tell you this, but you don't have a ghost in here."

"I don't? What in the hell do I have then?"

Mel walked to the middle of the large foyer and placed her hands on her hips and slowly moved her body around in a circle.

Edward's voice cut through her concentration. "What are you doing, Mel?"

"Creating a specter radar." The men stared at her dumbstruck.

Now, that's a look I've seen before. She smiled to herself.

Josh frowned. "What do you mean about no ghost and what's a specter radar?"

Mel nodded. "It's something like a human compass for the

paranormal. I'm sorry to tell you Edward that you don't have one ghost. You have at least four ghosts haunting your house."

Lenny's eyes bulged. "Holy shit! We're dead meat."

His face flushed with embarrassment, as he looked at Mel. "Beg your pardon, Ma'am. My Mamma would whoop me with her wooden spoon if she knew that I'd sworn in front of a lady."

Mel smiled at him "Don't worry, Lenny. This sort of situation would make anybody lose their composure. Especially if you're not used to it."

Lenny smiled sheepishly. "I'm beholden to you, Ma'am."

"Please, I want you all to call me Mel."

Edward stared at her. "Did you say we have four ghosts haunting this place? What the hell are we going to do?" He reached for her as he asked.

When Edward took her hand, tiny electric sparks coursed up her arm from his touch.

"Can you help us, Mel? We've got a lot riding on this."

She jumped as another scream ripped through the air. The men didn't move, but they were visibly shaken.

The screaming surrounded them, so intense that it felt like their very bones vibrated from the piercing noise.

Mel pointed to the door. "I've had enough. Let's get out of here."

Edward stood on the sidewalk in front of the house. "You didn't answer my question Mel. Can you get rid of whatever is in there?"

Blowing air out between her lips, she said, "I'm going to try, Edward. I'll do the best I can do."

3

E dward cracked his lobster claw, removed the meat and dipped it in a small container of butter before Mel spoke.

"So, fill me in."

He waved a lobster fork at her. "Not before you try your first bite of lobster."

They sat in an old dancehall that served fabulous lobster suppers. It had taken half an hour to drive there from Lunenburg. Edward said he had chosen the place because they could talk undisturbed and have a fabulous dinner. They'd sampled the mussels and filled up on salad displayed in a large dory, before moving on to the next course.

She dipped her lobster in the melted butter and leaned over her plate so the butter wouldn't drip down over the red lobster printed on her plastic bib.

Her eyes opened wide in pleasant surprise. "Oh, my gosh. This is delicious."

Edward laughed at the expression on her face. "See, I said you'd like it."

She groaned. "Like it? I love it." She followed Edward's

lead and threw the shell into a large stainless-steel bowl on the wooden table.

"Now fill me in Edward and don't leave anything out. I need all the information you can give me to take down whatever it is in your house – and to keep it down."

He tore the tail of the lobster from its body. "Okay, this is what I found out."

The house originally belonged to an Archibald Ramey, a merchant and sea captain in Lunenburg. He owned three ships and because of his travels, he became a very wealthy man. He married the love of his life, but she died in childbirth."

"Oh, that's sad."

Edward nodded. "It is, but the babies survived."

"Babies?"

Edward nodded. "Yes, she gave birth to identical twins, Olive and Emma. The story goes that both girls were beautiful inside and out. They had a huge double wedding and most of Lunenburg came to celebrate with them. Archie built a new home with suites for both couples upstairs in the now said-to-be haunted house."

"Wow. Is that why the stairs split to the left and right after the stained-glass window?"

"It is. Huge living quarters with six bedrooms and sitting rooms. Word is, that he doted on those two girls. They were married at the same time, to two brothers, who captained two of Archie's frigates."

"What happened?"

She looked around at the shells strewn around on her plate, searching for another piece of lobster meat.

Edward roared with laughter at the look on her face.

"What? What's so funny?" she asked.

"I'm sorry for laughing Mel, but you should have seen the

disappointment on your face when you realized that you'd eaten the last of your lobster."

"I can't believe I ate it that fast." Her face reddened with embarrassment.

He grinned at her smugly. "The next time I tell you to order a two-pounder, you should listen."

He tore the second large claw from the body of his lobster and offered it to her.

Now she really was embarrassed. "I can't take that from you."

Silently, he reoffered the large claw.

She passed her plate over to him. "Okay... Give it to me. I'm not proud." She started cracking the shell. "That's twice, I'm eating a one-pound lobster."

"Twice?"

"Uh huh. The first and the last time."

Edward roared again. He had a warm, booming voice. Most people looked over and smiled at the handsome man who was obviously having a nice time.

She waved a succulent piece lobster meat in front of him. "Is there more to the story?"

He took a drink of his beer. "Well, as near as I can understand, the men sailed away and they hadn't been gone very long when the daughters were all killed by a disgruntled employee."

Mel shook her head in disbelief. "Wow, he must have been more than disgruntled."

The waitress arrived at their table with a grin on her face and reached for the bowl of shells. She emptied the shell bowl into a large container.

Their server's name tag read: Emma. The young woman, in her late thirties hovered around them. "How was the lobster?"

Mel nodded. "It was amazing. The next time I eat here I'm going to order the two-pounder."

Emma laughed. "Good for you. Help yourself to tea or coffee by the stage over there. I hope you saved room for dessert."

Mel sighed. "I don't think I have any room left."

"Yes, you do." Emma nodded her head and smiled, her hands on her hips. You can't come to the Shore Club without having one of our special desserts."

Edward smiled. "Let me order for you. Bring both of us the lemon dessert, please."

Mel put her hand up. "Oh, I really can't eat another mouthful."

Edward chuckled. "Was I right about the two-pound lobster?"

Mel sighed deeply. "Yes, you were. Bring the lemon thing on, Emma."

Before Emma left, Edward laid his hand on hers. "I find you a very fascinating woman, Mel. Where did the nickname Mel come from?" He quirked his eyebrow at her and her heart fluttered a little. She smiled to cover her reaction to his touch and gently pulled her hand from under his.

"My cousin, Kelsey, could only pronounce Mel when she was small, so that's how I got my nickname. It kinda stuck."

"So, what exactly is a ghostbuster?"

"Well, that's a good question."

Edward smiled. "I thought so. How about an answer?"

"Well, I think you need a short version of 'Ghostie 101'."

"Ghostie 101?"

Mel nodded her head. "You see, ghosts are the energy of people who have died – the ones that haven't crossed over."

"Crossed over?"

"*Mmm hmm*. Crossed over. I like to think that heaven is

their final stop, but for some reason they don't make it there. Now, take Flossie Ramey."

"Who?"

Mel smiled at him. "You know the woman that I helped cross over to be with her little girl, Edith?"

Edward stared at her. "You know that much about her?"

Mel smiled at his confusion. "Well yes. You see Flossie didn't know that she had died. And time stopped when she and her daughter were killed on the street by a team of runaway horses."

Edward took a sip of coffee. "So, time stands still?"

"Well for some of them, but for others, well they simply refuse to go into the light because they have unfinished business here on earth."

"Unfinished?"

Mel took a sip of her water and smiled to herself. Edward was beginning to sound like a parrot, a drop-dead-gorgeous parrot.

"By unfinished, I mean they have a journey and they haven't completed it yet. And only when they complete it are they ready to cross over."

She took another sip of water. "Then, there are the spirits like the one that Lenny had a confrontation with that will never see the light because they are pure evil. They stay here on this plane because they have a vendetta or something they feel a driving need to accomplish."

"So, when do they go 'to the light'?" He air quoted with his hands.

Mel shook her head. "They never see the light. They surround themselves with darkness and sometimes with destruction and that's where I come in – and others like me. I try to banish them to the dark underworld and keep them where they belong."

His eyes widened. "You mean hell?"

"That's one of the names for it."

"And you do this for a living?"

Mel smiled at the look of shock on his face. "Well, I wanted to be a brain surgeon, but I sucked at biology."

Edward roared with laughter. "I'm so glad you sucked at biology. What other talents do you have?"

"I'm not sure they're talents, but I can talk to the dead and sense when something paranormal is about to happen."

"Now that's interesting. Good or bad?"

"Both."

He stared at her, shaking his head.

Mel braced herself. *Here it comes. The ridicule. The disbelief.*

Edward inhaled deeply and took her hand again, caressing a tender knuckle with his thumb. "You are one amazing woman, Mel Gordon, and I would love to get to know you on a personal level. Do you think that could be possible?"

She took her hand back again and smiled sadly at Edward. I'd love to be your friend, but anything more... I'm afraid that's impossible right now."

He stared at her.

At this moment, she'd give up two lobster dinners just to be able to read his mind like her cousin, Kelsey, could.

He took her hand again and squeezed it. "Well, that's good for a start. I'll take it."

Edward looked around the room and leaned over closer to Mel. "So, back to my question. What do I have living in my house?"

Mel took her hands and clasped them in front of her and leaned in toward Edward. "From what I can gather, you have both of the above."

"What? Please say you're not serious."

Mel nodded and had to smile at the look on his face, in spite of herself. "I'm afraid I am serious. I felt good and bad energy when I stood inside the foyer."

Emma arrived with dessert.

Mel looked down at the swirling lemon sauce falling over a cream-filled layered cake.

She groaned. "I'm just going to run down to the beach and back to make room before I eat this."

He grinned at her, shaking his head. "You'd better not. It might not be here when you get back."

Later, when every crumb of the lemon cake had disappeared, she placed her fork down and sighed with satisfaction.

"Now, Edward, it's your turn. Tell me some more about what I'm up against."

He took a drink of his coffee. "Well the stories vary. It's almost a legend in Lunenburg and the stories change slightly depending on who you speak to. There seem to be quite a few different slants on the tragedy. It happened..."

Mel interrupted. "Don't tell me *where*, Edward, I have to discover that for myself."

"Okay, that's not really a problem, because I don't exactly know. As I said, there've been so many stories about what happened that it's woven into the history of the place, but I know that it happened in the house. And the man was an Ian McGregor."

Mel wiped her hands again with the packaged wipes supplied by the waitress.

"Okay, so now that I know where, give me some background."

"Well, Archie Ramey was the last man in the town to give this Ian McGregor a job – others avoided hiring him because of his drinking. He wasn't a nice man – and that's being polite. So, Archie gave him a job delivering the merchandise from his stores. Well, the story goes that McGregor hit the bottle one day and raced the horses down Lincoln Street – which is where we're staying – killing a woman and her child."

Mel gasped. "Oh, how awful. Oh my gosh Edward, I think that was the woman that I helped cross over in front of our B&B."

He nodded his head, but Mel could tell that he didn't quite grasp what it meant to cross over.

"Well, Archie fired him and made sure that no one else hired him. His wife left him, taking their child with her. Apparently, he was very free with his fists. They say that Archie gave her a place to hide from McGregor."

"What a horrible man."

Edward nodded. "I'll say, he blamed Archie for all his troubles in every tavern around and people heard him threaten revenge on Archie. The coward waited until all the men of Archie's household had left on their voyage to England. He snuck into the house, murdered the servants, intending to kill the two people that Archie Ramey loved most in the world – his two daughters, who were both pregnant at the time."

"Oh my gosh, that's horrible. What happened to him? Did he hang for that horrendous crime?"

"No, sadly he didn't. He slit his throat after he killed the twins."

Emma arrived with the bill and placed it on the table between them. Mel went to take it, but Edward snapped it from the table.

She scolded him. "Edward, I told you that I wanted to take you out for dinner tonight."

He shook his head. "I know you did. I did not intend for you to pay this evening. I allowed you to think that, so you'd come and have dinner with me. There won't be any paying for dinner while you're working for my production company."

"Well, I just wanted to find out some more information about Archie Ramey and I always take my clients out for dinner."

Edward quirked his eyebrows, which did something silly to her tummy.

"Not this client. Anyway, that's all I can tell you about Archie Ramey and his family."

Emma, their waitress, gave a start and tried not to look at either of them when she processed the bill with the debit machine.

Mel sensed Emma was concerned about something.

"Emma, is something wrong?"

Embarrassed, she apologized to Mel. "I'm sorry, I didn't mean to listen to your conversation, but are you talking about the Ramey murders at the turn of the century?"

Surprised, Mel nodded. "Yes, we are. Why?"

Emma sighed. "That's my family you're talking about."

"Your family?" Edward looked around at the almost empty restaurant. "Can you sit down for a few moments?"

She smiled. "Oh sure. Just let me give the bill to that couple over in the corner and then I'll be right back."

In no time at all, she was sitting next to Mel and across from Edward.

She placed her hands on the table. "Now, what would you like to know?"

Mel looked at her. "Well for starters, how are you related?"

"Well, Archie Ramey had a sister, Annie. She was my great-grandmother. He was fifteen years older than her and from what she wrote, she adored him. He was well respected in the town of Lunenburg and beyond. She blamed herself for what happened to the girls that day."

Mel sat back and watched her. "Why?"

"Well, according to her journal, she was supposed to spend the day with the twins, Emma and Olive, but she fell and twisted her ankle and was laid up for a few days."

Edward took a drink of coffee. "Ironic, isn't it?"

Emma quizzed him. "What do you mean?"

"Well, if she hadn't hurt her ankle, you wouldn't be here sitting with us today."

"Gosh, I never really thought of that."

She looked at Mel. "You know that they were both pregnant at the time?"

Mel nodded. "Yes, Edward just told me. How do you know so much about what happened?"

"My great-grandmother, Annie, wrote everything down in her journal. Great-uncle Archie's ships were making one last stop in Nova Scotia, up the coast in Liverpool to pick up some cargo before heading for London, England. The bodies of his daughters were discovered the same day the murders happened. They sent word to Liverpool by land and the men left their ships, traveling back to Lunenburg by stage coach. The bodies had been removed by the time they arrived. They found the house in shambles, from the cellar to the attic."

Mel was impressed. "Wow, you really seem to know the facts."

Emma smiled at the mesmerized couple staring at her. "I should. I read Great-grandmother Annie's journal enough when I was younger. I'll tell you something else no one knows about Annie. She begged her brother not to sail off that day because she felt something bad was going to happen."

Mel leaned closer. "She did? What happened after they returned, Emma?"

"It was horrible. The double funeral so close after a double wedding. The entire town of Lunenburg went into mourning." She sighed. "It was too much for uncle Archie. He became ill and within the year, he died. The doctor said it was consumption."

Edward raised his eyebrows. "Consumption?"

Emma looked over at him. "Tuberculosis, but Gran Annie

said he died of a broken heart. He couldn't go on living any longer without his girls."

Mel touched the woman's hand. "Oh Emma, how sad."

"It really was."

Mel looked at Emma's name tag: "You wouldn't be named after one of the twins, would you?"

Emma smiled sadly. "I am. After both. My name is Emma Olive Annie Ramey."

Edward quizzed her. "Emma, how can you be a Ramey?"

Emma smiled. Because, my Gran Annie married a distant cousin who was a Ramey and ever since, there's been an Emma Olive Annie Ramey in every generation of our Ramey family."

Mel stared at her. "It's amazing that you have so much information."

Edward straightened up in his chair. "You say that there's a journal? How hard would it be to have a look at it?"

Emma shook her head. "Not hard at all. I own it. And I've almost memorized it."

Mel looked at her. "Really?"

"Yes, every generation of Emma Olive has been given the journal to safeguard for the next Emma Olive. I'm the next Emma after my grandmother. She had three boys and one of those was my father, so I was the next one in line."

Edward folded his receipt and placed it in his wallet. "Why do you need to safeguard it, Emma?"

She shook her head. "I don't really know. I guess the journal is the history of that horrible happening and Great-gran thought the memory of it needed to stay alive in our family."

Mel was hesitant, but she had to ask. "Emma do you think that I could have a look at the journal?"

Emma smiled. "Sure, I don't mind."

Edward glanced at his watch. "Emma, we want to thank

you for your generosity sharing all your information. We'll take you up on your offer to let us look at the journal. Where can we reach you?"

She pulled out a pad from her apron and wrote down some words and numbers, tore it off and passed it to Edward.

"You can reach me at this number, anytime. If I don't answer, just leave a message."

He took the paper and smiled. "Thank you, we'll be calling you very soon."

As Emma left their table, Edward noticed a pensive look on Mel's face.

"What's wrong?"

"There's something that Emma's not telling us**.**"

"What do you mean?"

"I sense that there's more to the story."

"Sense something?"

"Oh, didn't I tell you that was one of my other *umm*...gifts."

"You mean, she's lying?"

Mel shook her head. "Oh no, I don't mean that she's deceptive. I mean that she's not telling us the whole story. Maybe she doesn't know."

"That's interesting. Do you think it's connected to what's happening at the house?"

"Oh, without a doubt. It centers around the house and the murders."

"Well, we'll never know for sure."

Mel smiled at Edward as they rose to leave. "That's where you're wrong. We'll know very shortly."

"How do you know?"

"Because, I can find out."

4

Mel stood inside the foyer of the house. It was quiet. A spectral stillness lingered in the air. Not only lingered, but filled every nook and cranny of the house with memories that had not been erased or dealt with for a long time.

In front of her, the wide mahogany staircase swept up eight steps to the first landing, where the stairs split, turning left and right to the upper levels. The morning sun filtered through three stunning twelve-foot, stained glass windows that depicted a beautiful angel dressed in a snowy white robe with a vast wing span that back dropped the angel and filled the entire window area. The artist had filled her face with such sadness that it almost took Mel's breath away.

"Oh, how beautiful." Mel moved across the foyer to study the window more closely. The angel's hands were crossed at her breast. Realistic tears, painted on the glass, flowed down her face.

"Good morning, Mel."

She jumped and squealed, holding her hand to her chest. "Edward, you scared the life out of me."

"I'm sorry, Mel. I thought you heard me when I came in."

She laughed, a little embarrassed. "I'm afraid that when I'm deep in thought, I tune out everything except what I'm scanning for."

"Scanning?" He quirked his brow.

Mel couldn't help smiling. She wondered if Edward knew how sexy he was when he did that.

"Scanning is a term we use at the Gordon Agency when we're trying to locate the source – where a specter originates from. In this situation, that means where the actual murder took place."

Edward smiled. "Well that's not a problem. I can tell you that. I found out last night."

Mel put up her hand to stop him. "No, please don't. I must do this myself. I can feel the vibes; they're very strong."

"You mean a ghost is still here?"

She grinned at him. "You called me, right?"

He nodded his head and grinned sheepishly at her. "But, after all this time, why is it still so strong?"

She shrugged her shoulders. "Who knows? You have a very mean specter here."

"Great. You made my day."

"Edward, I can still feel the hatred in the air and it's lingering a long time after Lenny had his encounter with a very pissed off ghost. This one is strong. One of the strongest I've had to deal with since I started working with the Gordon Agency – and I've been there a long time."

She caught the look that crossed Edward's face.

"Don't worry. I can do it. But, it's going to be a challenge."

Edward dug his hands in his pocket. "I hope you can. We're running out of time. If we don't start production soon, we won't be ready for the season and we'll lose a lot of our advertisers. And some backers."

Mel sighed. "How long do I have?"

"Three weeks, maybe just a little more. Then we have to start taping again."

Mel was shocked. "Three weeks?"

He sighed deeply. "As executive producer, I have to make the decision to keep going or pull the plug. We must start filming here, so we can make the fall lineup, or we're washed up for this season. This year is important because of the movie's success. If the entertainment reporters hear about any of this, it could ruin the chances of the series becoming a hit. So, the sooner you get rid of whatever is here, the happier I'm going to be."

While Edward spoke, Mel walked through the dining room, toward the swinging, ornate double doors that led to the kitchen. She pushed through the doors and cold, dank air swirled around her. Waves of nausea swept through her body. Mel leaned against the doorframe, her face deathly pale.

Edward, following close behind, caught her before she collapsed to the floor.

He asked, his face, full of concern: "Mel, are you alright? What the hell just happened?"

She put out her hand, nodded and leaned against him.

He helped her to the first chair in the dining room. She sat down and smiled weakly up at Edward, who hovered over her.

"Sit down, you're giving me a crick in my neck."

He sat on a chair beside her. "What's wrong? Should I call an ambulance or take you to emergency?"

"No, I'm fine. It happened in the kitchen, didn't it?"

He nodded, his face still full of concern.

Edward looked at her with respect. "You're right. It was the kitchen."

"I had to find out where it started. She laughed sheepishly. Boy, did I ever."

He took both her hands in his. She didn't pull away and his felt warm and comforting.

"Will you be okay, Mel? Your color is finally returning. You were as white as a sheet."

She could feel her face blush as he rubbed her hands with his thumbs. She really enjoyed having his hands hold hers, but she eased them out from under his and folded them on her lap.

Mel smiled weakly at him. "I'm fine. Thanks for being there to catch me." She looked around, taking in the details of his home. "Wow, what a beautiful home."

He followed her gaze. "It is, isn't it? That's what I thought when I bought it."

"You bought it?"

He nodded. "I did. That's another reason why I want this to end. I plan to live here for at least half of my working year."

She looked around. "And you're only giving me three weeks to finish this job?"

"Sorry, Mel, that's all the time I have."

She stood up and looked around. "Well then, I guess it's time for me and mean Mr. Ghostie to come out from our corners, fighting."

She looked at Edward with determination. "And I'm going to win."

5

E dward slowed the car down. "We're in luck. There's a parking spot."

Mel sighed in contentment, watching the waves roll across Hubbard's beach. "What a beautiful evening. I'm so glad you invited me for dinner."

Edward chuckled. "Well, I know how much you enjoyed the lobster dinner here at the Shore Club and after this morning I think I owe you another one."

Later, when the very last crumb of lemon cake was consumed, Mel put her fork down and sighed. "Wow, I think that was even better than the last meal we had here – and that was amazing."

She noticed that the tables around them were being placed against the walls. Musicians arrived and placed instruments against stools that stood on the small stage in the front of the dining room. "I wonder what's going on?"

Edward leaned closer and she caught a hint of his spicy cologne.

"They're getting ready for the dance. They have one every Saturday night. Would you like to stay?"

Mel panicked. "Oh, I don't think so. I haven't danced in a very long time. I was always told that I had two left feet."

Edward snorted. "I can't believe that. Come on; it will be fun."

Mel placed a hand on his arm. "No really. I can't dance." She sighed. "Let's just sit here and listen."

Edward smiled at her. "Okay, that sounds good, for now."

The music was great. Mel, who loved all music, felt herself swaying to the old pop classics of the sixties. Someone dimmed the lights and Edward took her hand.

"They're playing 'Ebb Tide'. It's one of my old favorites."

Mel shook her head and panicked. "No really, I can't."

Edward smiled. "Come on Mel, dance with me. I'm going to look very silly out there twirling around on my own."

She laughed and nodded. "Oh alright, but remember I warned you."

He took her arm and led her to the dance floor, placed his arms around her waist and gently pulled her against his body. They moved as one with the music. Mel was in heaven.

Edward looked down at her.

She sighed. "This is so nice."

Edward murmured into her hair. "It certainly is."

She rested her head on his shoulder. "I haven't danced since my engagement party and then I almost broke David's foot."

Edward stopped abruptly. "Engagement party?" He held her hand up, studied her ring finger and started moving around the floor again. "I don't see any ring."

She shook her head. "No, I gave it back to him when he called off our wedding."

He twirled her around. Though the conversation had veered in a direction she hadn't chosen, Mel still felt as if she were dancing on air.

"All I can say is that it's his loss, Mel."

"You can say that again. He is a total jerk."

Edward tilted his head back and laughed. "That's the attitude for a jilted bride to have. Good for you."

He held her tighter and Mel realized that she had missed out on so much with David. Her body began to vibrate against Edward's and that shocked her. They both started to laugh when Edward took his phone from his breast pocket.

He grinned. "Sorry. My phone." The music stopped and they returned to the table with Edward speaking into his cell as he walked.

"Evening Josh. What? When?" Edward sighed deeply. "Okay, we're at the Shore Club. We'll be there in twenty minutes."

"What happened, Edward?"

"Our ghost has struck again."

Mel grabbed her purse from the table. "Edward, I need to go there now."

"Okay." He grabbed her hand and pulled her through the crowd on the dance floor.

Twenty minutes later, they arrived at the Ramey mansion. Every window facing the street shone with light. Josh paced back and forth in front of the main entrance and ran toward their vehicle as they parked at the curb.

Edward jumped out with Mel close behind him. "What happened?"

Josh stood there shaking his head in disbelief. "Man, you're not going to believe this, but every piece of furniture in the two front rooms has been destroyed."

"That can't be possible." Edward stared over at Mel incredulous. "Can it?"

She nodded. "I'm afraid so. Edward, your problem is even worse than what I thought it was." Mel moved up the steps to the front entrance of the house. Edward followed close behind her. She turned and faced him, crossing her arms and standing her ground.

"Stay out, Edward. Let me go in there by myself. Give me ten minutes then you can come in."

A muscle throbbed on the side of Edward's jaw. "It's too dangerous. I can't let you go in there by yourself." He placed his hands on his hips. "That's just not going to happen."

Mel sighed and took Edward's hand. "No, I'll be okay. It probably used all its energy doing the damage, so we won't hear from it anymore tonight. It takes a lot of energy to do what Josh said it did. Isn't this what you hired me for? I'm a ghostbuster. Remember?"

Edward smiled, looking down at their hands and frowned as she pulled her hand away. He cleared his throat. "For now, you're my ghostbuster and I don't want anything to happen to you. So, work around that because going in alone is not an option."

She sighed. "Okay, let's compromise. I'll go in and you stay by the front entrance, just inside the foyer."

"No. I'm going with you. Wherever you go."

Mel's pissed-off meter was close to steaming on the dial.

"Look. Let me do my job. I do it well and I don't need babysitters."

She placed her hands on her hips and glared at him. "I'm allowing you to go into the house with me, on my terms. Take it or leave it."

They stared at each other. Finally, he nodded. "But, if there's one thing inside that I don't like, I want you out of there. Is that understood?"

Mel shook her head. "I can't work like that. If I think I'm in danger, I'll leave. I promise."

He stood there, the pulse still throbbing at his jaw. "Okay, let's go."

Frustrated, Mel pointed to the men standing on the bottom step. "You guys go home or get a beer or something."

They didn't budge, but watched Edward for direction.

Mel could feel her face burning with anger.

Edward sighed deeply. "Okay guys, let's listen to the ghostbuster lady. Get a beer. I'll call you if I need you."

Reluctantly, they left, but not before giving Mel one last look, hoping she'd change her mind.

Edward opened the front door for her and followed Mel into the foyer. They stood rooted to the spot and stared. The dining room chairs had been thrown and were broken into pieces against the base of the walls. What was left of a beautiful Sheridan table and buffet lay upside down on the floor. Large oil paintings of ships, in ornate frames, had been smashed over the back of chairs.

Edward took a deep breath. "What the hell happened?"

Mel grabbed his arm. "Edward, you've got one pissed off ghost here. And I'm going to find out why."

He sighed. "Well, when you do, ask him if he has insurance. I'm not sure my policy covers ghost destruction."

Mel stared at him. "Your furniture is wrecked and your priceless pictures are destroyed and your beautiful antique furniture is now no better than kindling for the fireplace and you can joke about your insurance policy? Look at that beautiful Sheridan side table. It's totally ruined."

Edward took her arm. "I am upset, but what's the use of ranting and raving? It won't bring them back."

Mel sighed. "But all that beautiful Sheridan furniture. Those were the first ones I'd really seen except on the *Antique Roadshow*."

He cocked his head. "I gather you like old furniture."

"No, I love old furniture and old homes. It's a passion I share with my cousin, Kelsey, and my Aunt Jo."

"Well, when we finish here, I'll take you to a warehouse

I've rented in town and show you the furniture you love so much." He grinned at her. "I'll even let you touch it."

"Touch it?"

Edward nodded and gestured to the broken furniture. "These were replica pieces I had made for the movie. I didn't want anything to happen to the real antiques on set."

She placed her hand on her chest. "Oh, thank goodness. What a wonderful idea you had."

He grinned at her. "I thought so. I love old furniture too. Let's go. We can't do anything else—"

Mel interrupted him. "*Shhhhh*, listen. Do you hear that?"

Edward tilted his head and listened. "I don't hear anything. In fact, it's dead quiet in here."

Mel looked at him and smiled. "Really? Dead silence? How can you joke at a time like this? Though a very bad one, it's a joke nonetheless."

He smiled. "It was the best I could do on such short notice."

She held her hand up again. "Listen. Do you hear that?"

Edward shook his head. "No, I don't hear a thing."

Mel heard it again. "It's definitely someone crying."

"Crying? You're kidding. Right?"

"No, I'm not kidding."

Mel moved further into the foyer. Her attention focused on the staircase. Around the sweeping staircase, swirling moist air moved back and forth and danced around, uniting into a denser mass on the second step of the stairs. Mel watched as the twirling air formed a huddled figure of a little girl. She sat sobbing into a transparent apron she held up to her face with both hands.

Mel whispered to Edward. "Stay here and don't say a word."

She walked over and up-righted a chair from the floor –

one that hadn't been destroyed – sat down, cleared her mind and spoke telepathically.

"Hello. Are you okay?" The crying continued and Mel tried again.

"Hello...can I help you?"

The little ghost huddled against the bannister for protection.

Mel tried again. *"My name is Melissa. What's your name?"*

She waited with bated breath, hoping to connect with this little ghost that was sobbing her heart out.

"I really want to help you. Let me help you, please. Can you tell me your name?"

From a distance Mel heard one word that made her heart sing.

"Ka-Katie."

No matter how many times Mel contacted a specter, it was always a surprise when something like this actually happened.

"Katie? What a pretty name. You can call me Mel, Katie, I want to help you so bad. What happened here?"

"Jesus, Mary and Joseph. It's him. The monster from hell. He's back." The little girl hugged the banister and sobbed again. Even so, Katie came in loud and clear.

"Him? Monster from Hell? What do you mean?"

"That he is. That McGregor beast. He left and now he's back. The Blessed Virgin Mother protect us. He's back. We all run from him and hide when he comes. Holy Mother of God, I'm so afraid because he's back."

Mel tried to make her telepathic voice as soothing as she could, but all she wanted to do was ask questions. She knew from experience, that if she rushed this terrified specter, she would have no answers to all the questions that were bubbling up inside her.

"Katie, you don't have to stay. You can leave. I'll guide you to a

wonderful, beautiful place where he can never hurt you. No one will ever be able to hurt you again."

Katie started to cry again softly. "I... I can't...go. Me missus, they...needs me. He searches and searches and he gets mad...der and madder."

Katie started to fade as she spoke to Mel. *"I have to go hide from him. You should hide before he comes back...looking."*

Frustrated, Mel almost shouted out loud. *"Katie wait. What is he looking for?"*

Katie began to fade from the sweeping staircase.

"I have to hide now. He won't rest long. He'll be searching again soon."

"Katie wait. What is he searching for?"

The little ghost faded out of sight completely, but not before Mel thought she heard the word... "gold".

————

Edward stood by the door and watched. His jaw dropped. What the hell was sitting on the stairs huddled against the banister? Swirling smoke? His eyes widened when he realized that it was a form, a very loose, transparent form of a girl crouched on the stairs in front of Mel.

Amazed, he watched as Mel sat and stared at the stairs. He moved closer to get a better look. When Mel noticed what he was doing, her hand raised abruptly and she shook her head quickly for him to stop. He did. Leaning back against one of the pillars in the foyer, he watched as her hands moved, as if in a conversation with whatever it was on the stairs. Who the hell was she talking to?

He watched Mel pull her hair back into a ponytail and then let it cascade over her shoulders again, without realizing what she was doing. The more he saw of Mel Gordon, the more he was convinced that he was going to find out what made this beautiful woman tick. She had built a wall around her. He was going to take that wall down one brick at a time, if it was the last thing he did. He chuckled to himself. It might take a while to wear Mel down, but he knew one thing for sure, one day he would take that girl home to meet his grandmother.

6

Mel rose from her chair and joined Edward where he leaned against the marble pillars in the grand foyer, his arms crossed.

Her look was pensive. Edward moved to meet her halfway. "Mel, tell me what that was all about?"

"I will, but first I need coffee, and lots of it."

He took her arm and opened the door. "There's a place down the next street. It's still open." He guided them toward his car.

Mel shook her head. "No, I want to walk because I don't want anyone listening to our conversation."

Intrigued, he nodded. "Then let's go this way." They walked down the street past lovely old turn-of-the-century homes.

She sighed. "I love Lunenburg. I could really live here."

Edward laughed. "That's how I feel about this area as well." He took her arm as they crossed a busy intersection. People passed them with cameras hanging around their necks and guide books rolled up in their hands or sticking out of backpacks.

"Wow, there are a lot of tourists around this evening."

"It's like this all summer long. Now tell me what has your forehead all puckered up?"

Mel stopped and touched her head. "Puckered? Really?"

He laughed at her expression. "No, not really, but I know there's something on your mind and you have to tell me right now. What happened back at the house just now, and who was that on the stairs?"

"Mel stopped and stood in front of Edward. "Wait. You could see someone on the stairs?"

He nodded. "I could. It looked like a little girl."

She eyed Edward. "That's very interesting. A lot of people can't see specters, even when they become solid."

He shrugged. "I'm sure a lot of people can see them. Now give me the full deal. I want every word."

"Well, her name is Katie and I gather that she was killed in the house all those years ago. And it is McGregor that's causing all the damage. All the spirits in the house are terrified of him. I tried to help Katie to cross over, but she won't go without her mistresses."

She stopped and took a closer look at St. John's Anglican Church.

"How beautiful." She smiled at him. "Did I tell you how much I love Lunenburg?"

He grinned. "I think you did — several times — now tell me more. What did Katie tell you that made your forehead wrinkle?"

She glared at him. "Hey."

Edward laughed. "Sorry, I meant pensive looking."

Mel laughed. "That's better. Well, I don't know how to tell you this, but McGregor's on a rampage because he's looking for something."

Edward stopped, turned and stared at her.

"He's looking for something? What's he looking for?"

Mel shrugged. "Katie was fading, but I'm sure that I heard the word...'gold'."

"Gold. Are you sure?"

"No, I'm not. She had just about faded when I heard the word. I think we need to get in touch with Emma and take a look at her grandmother's diary."

"I think that's an excellent idea."

"Edward, I need to know when things started happening at the house."

"Okay, I'll check with Josh. He's kept everything documented. I knew we had a few small problems when we were shooting the movie, but after we lined everything up for the pilot for the T.V. series, that's when things hit the fan."

"What kind of problems?"

"Oh, during the making of the movie, we'd feel something touch us, mostly our backs or legs and we'd hear voices. But then the damage started taking place and the little taps on the back turned into pushes." Edward stood in front of the coffee shop. "I have Emma's number and I think it's time we had a look at Great-grandmother Annie's journal."

———

Emma placed coffee on the kitchen table in front of them. Steam from a basket of blueberry muffins filled the air with a delicious aroma. They sat in front of a garden window and gazed out over the back harbor of Lunenburg.

Mel looked around. "What a beautiful home, Emma."

"It is, isn't it? It's not as grand as yours, Edward, but this house has been in the family for over a hundred years. My great-grandfather, Angus Ramey, built it for his bride, my great-gran Annie and over the years different family members made changes to make this house their own. When I inherited it, we realized that it needed larger windows to look over the back harbor. My husband, Bruce, took the wall out and put in wall-to-wall garden windows."

She pointed to the rain falling outside. "If it was fine, we'd be sitting on the patio."

She placed her mug on the table and smiled at them. "But, I'm sure you didn't come to hear about Bruce's wonderful carpentry skills."

Mel sighed and shook her head, wondering what was the easiest way to approach the subject of ghosts to Emma.

"Emma, some information came to light that might have a bearing on what's happening at the house. We think it might have something to do with your great-grandmother's journal."

Emma took a muffin and buttered it. "What kind of information?"

Mel paused, trying to find the right words, but Edward jumped in before she could stop him.

"Did you ever hear about any gold or treasure being hidden at the house?"

Unconcerned, Emma smiled. "That was always the rumor. My great-uncle Archie had a few quirks and one of them was going to great lengths to ensure the safety of his money."

Emma leaned forward. "Safety?"

"Yes, the story goes that some men came from Halifax by stage coach and robbed the bank. They stole a lot of money and some of it belonged to Archie. So, according to family legend, he began stashing his money away." She shrugged. "But, it doesn't make a lot of sense that he put it in the house. He had a large vault at his store and if he was going to put it anywhere, he would have placed it there for safe keeping."

Mel looked over at the view. "Emma, I feel that your journal has information that could help with what's taking place in Edward's house now."

"The journal? There isn't anything written in it that says anything about a treasure."

Mel took a deep breath. *Here goes.* "Now Emma, I don't want you to think I'm crazy, but I spoke to a ghost recently and she told me that there's a spirit that's been doing all the damage at the house because it's looking for something."

"You were speaking to a ghost?"

Mel shook her head. "I know it sounds crazy to you, but I was."

"Oh, that has to be Katie."

Mel sat straight up in her chair. "What? How did you know it was Katie?"

"Oh, my grannie used to talk to her all the time when she played at the big house. That's what the family always called your house, Edward."

Edward rolled his eyes. "Your grandmother could talk to the dead?"

Mel smiled at Edward's reaction. "That would be your grandmother, Emma Olive. Right?"

Emma nodded and grinned. "That's right, another Emma Olive Annie Ramey."

He glanced at his watch. "Emma, I know that this is a very huge favor to ask, but do you think we could take the journal for a day and study it. I promise we'll guard it with our lives."

She shook her head and walked to the ceiling-high, oak bookcases standing behind them. "No, I'm sorry, I can't do that. We were told never to let it out of our sight."

Edward caught the acute disappointment that clouded Mel's face as she sighed and smiled at Emma. "We understand."

Emma reached for a file folder on a shelf. "When you called, I knew you'd want to look at it, so I copied the complete journal for you."

Mel was shocked by Emma's generosity. "Oh my gosh, Emma. Are you sure? Thank you so much."

Emma grinned. "Well, we were told never to leave it out of our sight, but nobody said we couldn't photocopy it and give it to someone to read."

Edward took her hand and shook it. "This is very generous of you, Emma. There's something I've wondered about. What happened to the house after the tragedy?"

"Well, it was only my great-gran and Archie left in the family. They had brothers and sisters, but they all died from diphtheria at a young age, leaving only Annie and Archie. So, when Archie died, he left everything he had to my great-gran, Annie."

"Everything?"

"Yes everything. Over the years, she tried to move her family into the big house, but they kept coming back here to live. They always kept your place up too, in memory of the family. The last to inherit it was my sister and myself. We decided to finally sell it."

Edward was shocked. "Are you saying that I bought the house from you?"

"Well, from both of us, through our lawyers. Linda lives in Vancouver and I didn't want it. I love it here in my house."

He smiled at Emma. "So that's how I was able to buy the house and all the land."

"That's right. Lock, stock and barrel."

Mel looked confused.

Emma laughed at her. "It means everything comes with it."

————

The next morning, Mel and Edward ran into each other outside their rooms on the landing.

"Good morning Mel. Going for breakfast?"

"You bet. I have no willpower and wouldn't miss pancakes

smothered in maple syrup, with sausages and bacon and Lunenburg hash browns on the side."

Edward stopped and stared at her. "And you know we're having this because...?"

Mel laughed at the look on his face.

"I'm not the psychic, that's my cousin Kelsey. I just called down to see what was on the menu for breakfast. I'm starved. I was up half the night reading the journal."

He stood back so Mel could take the stairs first. "In that case, let's indulge in the culinary delight you just described, and then fill me in on the journal."

They sat over coffee and Mel wished she had ordered the small breakfast instead of the "Fisherman's Deluxe." They weren't kidding when the menu said it was hearty.

She pulled her leg back underneath the chair. The next time, she would choose the table. The small table was just a little too cozy for her peace of mind. Their knees almost intertwined. Nice, but awkward and embarrassing...but still nice.

After the waitress came along and topped-up their coffees, Edward leaned back and looked at her. "Okay. What did you find when you read Annie's journal?"

Mel sipped her delicious brew and placed the cup down on the table. "Well, I can tell you this, there's something more going on in that journal than just the recounting of what happened after Archie lost his daughters in that horrendous murder. Annie writes that after the girls were killed, Archie had an artist design the stained-glass window with the weeping angel in the likeness of the twins."

"Are you saying that the angel looks like the twins?"

Mel nodded. "That's right. Archie had a portrait of the girls painted before they were married. The designer of the stain glass window used that likeness for the face of the angel."

Edward whistled. "They were stunning women."

Mel nodded and smiled. "Yes, if the angel is anything to go by. That window meant a lot to Annie because she felt close to her nieces every time she looked at it."

She took another sip of her coffee. "And get this. The artist he hired to create the window was from Boston."

"Boston? That's a little strange isn't it, when Halifax is less than a hundred miles away?"

"I thought so. That's basically all I learned from the diary. I just find it odd that he hired someone all the way from Boston. At that time, it was a long way for an artist to travel."

As she spoke, Edward leaned forward and casually draped his arm over the back of her chair, touching her neck in the process.

His phone rang. He looked at the screen and frowned. "I have to go, Mel. Remember we're meeting for lunch at the Grand Banker on Montague Street."

She nodded and smiled. "I'll meet you there, but first I have to go to the hardware store."

Mel sighed as she watched him leave. Edward was a nice man, but she wasn't sure if she was ready for another relationship. She had to put the brakes on her emotions because Edward appealed to her a lot.

He was everything that jerk, David, wasn't. Just the touch of his hand felt wonderful, but she was afraid to give her heart to another man. Her gifts were unique, but in the eyes of most men she had encountered and considered having a relationship with, she was a freak. She could only hope that someday she would be lucky enough to find someone like Jake, her Cousin Kelsey's husband. But she thought that only happened in fairy tales and it would be against the odds that two freaks in the same family could be so lucky in love.

———

Mel left the hardware store loaded down with all the magnets she could find. She looked up and down the street, trying to remember where Edward said that they would meet. Where was that damn restaurant?

Someone down the street shouted her name. She turned her head in that direction. It was Edward. She waved and joined him on the other side of the street.

He grinned. "I thought I should wait for you because with all the one-way streets, you might not find your way until lunch was over."

She laughed. "I'm famous in my family for my bad sense of direction. So, thanks."

They entered a large room completely walled-in with glass on the water side. Josh and Dan waved to them from a table tucked in a corner overlooking the harbor.

Edward pointed to where the guys sat. "I booked a secluded corner table to give us some privacy."

When she reached the table, Lenny stood up. Dan and Josh followed his lead.

Edward sat down and motioned to the waitress. "Let's order and then we'll start our meeting."

After they ordered, their drinks arrived. Edward leaned forward and lowered his voice.

"We have three weeks to get rid of whatever this thing is that's making my home a living hell. Now, if any of you decide that you don't want to continue to work for Lone Mountain Productions on this project, I understand. I'll assign you to another location and then we can move on. I must ask that you keep whatever happened, and happens here, under wraps, until Mel can get rid of whatever it is."

She cleared her voice. "I think I know who it is, Edward."

All heads turned in her direction. "It's McGregor, the man that killed Archie's two daughters and the two servants in your home all those years ago."

Mel watched Lenny's Adam's apple bob nervously in his throat, as he swallowed. "Why do you think it's him, ma'am?"

"Because one of the other ghosts told me, Lenny."

She loved the look of shock that hit their faces as she looked around the table. Shock and disbelief. Mainly disbelief. She'd seen it so many times before.

Josh put his hand up. "Whoa, whoa, just a minute. Other ghosts? You've got to be kidding."

She nodded at them. "I'm not kidding. Other ghosts. I think that there are five spirits or what you call ghosts. Five that still remain, or as you would say, haunt the house. I detect two strong personalities and the other three are very weak. McGregor is very strong and bad...very bad."

Edward began to speak, but Mel raised her hand to interrupt him.

"All I'm saying is that this McGregor character wasn't all peaches and cream when he was alive and he has become a lot worse since he died. And..." She looked around at the men. "He's going to get a lot worse."

Edward blew air out through his lips and searched all the faces around the table. "So, that leads me back to the first question I asked a little while ago. If any of you want to leave, I quite understand. Especially you, Lenny."

Josh cleared his throat. "I'm staying. I want to see this through."

Dan sighed. "That goes for me too. How much worse can it get?"

Lenny nodded to Mel. "I'd like to stay on. I'm not saying I'm all that plucky about it, but I want to see this to the end too. I'm not a quitter, ma'am."

She smiled. "I know you're not, Lenny, and will you please stop calling me ma'am. Mel is fine."

He nodded at her and smiled sheepishly.

Edward took a drink of coffee. "I want to thank all of you

for this. You're the best of the best and if there's any way we can accomplish what we need to do before the deadline, you're the ones who can do it, ghosts or no ghosts." Edward lifted his glass. "A toast: Down the hatch and down with ghosts."

Everyone lifted their glass and repeated: "Down with ghosts."

Their food arrived and Mel enjoyed the best plate of fish and chips she had ever eaten. After the meal, she pushed back her plate, took a sip of iced tea and folding her hands in front of her, looked around the table.

"Now, it's my turn. I know this is going to be hard to believe, but you need to know I am always in charge of the investigations I decide to work on."

Edward began to speak, but Mel raised her hand to silence him again.

"I don't need to have someone in the house with me, when I go in." She looked over at Edward. "Unless I request assistance. This is my job and I have to follow certain procedures and having someone untrained, that I have to worry about, just doesn't sit well with me."

She paused and smiled at them. "I need to make sure that you all understand this. I have the last word. You need to agree on this, or I won't remain to work on this project."

A pulse throbbed at the corner of Edward's neck. "It's too dangerous for you to be in there by yourself, Mel."

She sighed. "It's my job Edward, it's what I've been trained to do. I have a success rate of ninety-eight percent."

She smiled at the look of concern on the faces staring at her. "I know what I'm doing, guys. Now, the best time for me to enter the house is twilight or a little before, so I'm hoping that by then you'll be finished whatever you're doing for the day." She placed her hands on the table and pushed the chair back, so she could leave. "I'm starting this evening at seven o'clock. Will you be done by then?"

Concern was etched on all their faces though they gave passable nods in her direction.

"I'm not being mean; I just want to keep you safe too. Now, can you point me toward another hardware store because I bought all the magnets in Lunenburg."

————

At twilight, armed with magnets secured in numerous pockets of her specially designed hoodie, Mel drove to the end of the cul-de-sac and parked behind Josh's van. All three guys were standing outside...waiting for her.

She grabbed her large sports bag from the back of the Jeep and dropped it on the sidewalk. After yanking out the recessed handle of the bag, she waved at them.

"Hi guys."

Dan walked down the front steps toward her, just as Edward pulled up behind Mel's SUV.

Edward got out and leaned against Mel's car, waiting for Josh, Dan and Lenny to join them.

Mel looked around and grinned. "You guys aren't ganging up on me, are you?"

Edward cleared his throat. "Here's the deal, Mel. We'll let you go in there alone, but the door must always be open and there will be at least one man waiting on the outside, in case you need some help. We decided this after you left the restaurant."

She could tell they were braced for any arguments she might hurl at them. Instead, she grabbed the suitcase handle and smiled.

"That sounds fine with me. I really appreciate it, guys. I can live with that."

Grinning, she dragged her bag past three stunned men toward the house and whatever waited for her inside.

Edward motioned to the men. "You can go back to the lab guys, I'll stay on the doorstep for this shift."

Mel opened the front door and listened. She moved further inside the vestibule and listened again. Silence. She took a deep breath and mumbled. "Where are the ghosties when you want them?"

Her glance traveled to the stained-glass window. "Oh, how beautiful." She watched as the last streaks of sunlight bathed the glass angel in soft muted colors, slowly fading as the sun set below the base of the angel's feet.

She moved to the middle of the vestibule, placed her hands on her hips and took a deep breath.

"Okay, what would keep a spirit quiet for so long and then out of the blue, start this horrendous act of destruction?"

"Are you speaking to me?"

Mel jumped and grabbed her chest.

Edward stood inside the door.

"Oh my gosh, Edward, you took five years off my life."

"Sorry Mel. I thought you were speaking to me."

She smiled at him. "No, I often think out loud. She shrugged. "I don't detect any presence here right now, so I may as well case the joint." She grinned at him. "It's safe. I don't detect a thing. You want to come in and check it out with me?"

He cocked his head to one side. "Are you sure?"

She nodded. "Yes, I'm sure. This time it's safe. I'm not doing any ghostbusting. I have to find out what's bringing that nasty piece of work back to where it doesn't belong."

Edward stepped in behind her. "I'm right behind you."

"Fine, let's go upstairs."

They walked up the wide, sweeping staircase to the

landing where the angel wept. Stairs continued to the left and right.

Edward stood next to her. "Which way, boss?"

She grinned at the term boss. "I think we'll go to the right."

He followed her, taking pictures of the destruction as they moved up the seven steps to the second story landing.

Mel stared down the long hall before them. An aged, polished hardwood floor ended at an inviting window seat at the far end.

"Wow, I had no idea this place was so huge."

He nodded. "The hall is ten feet wide and forty feet long. I had the floors restored before the movie."

"They look so nice and slippery." She leaned over and removed her shoes, laughing at Edward's puzzled look.

"I'm really glad that I wore socks today." She ran down the hall and slid on the smooth hardwood floors then collapsed, laughing, on the window seat at the end.

Still laughing, she pointed to Edward's shoes. "Take your shoes off and try this. It's awesome."

He grinned at her enthusiasm. "Thanks, but I think I'll pass."

They giggled as she slid back to Edward and he caught her in his arms. Then, without warning, he stared into her eyes, lowered his face to hers...and kissed her.

She clung to his arms, praying her knees didn't buckle beneath her.

Breathless, she looked up at him, smiling. "How come?"

Still holding her, he gazed into her eyes. "Well, when a beautiful ghostbuster slides into your arms, it's just a natural reaction to kiss her. I thought it went rather well, didn't you?"

She giggled. "I most certainly did."

Mel enjoyed having Edward's arms wrapped around her a little too much. From past experience, she knew a relationship between them wouldn't work... She reluctantly shrugged out of his embrace.

He passed her sneakers to her.

She giggled. "Party pooper."

He quirked his eyebrows. "I've been called worse."

She laughed out loud again. "Now, Edward, we have to explore the bedrooms."

Mel searched through the large empty rooms adorned with ornate fireplaces and elaborate wainscoting.

The only creatures roaming were little dust bunnies that scuttled out of their way.

"Wow, these rooms are huge." She stood in front of a double bay window. "Oh my gosh, look at the view from here."

Edward joined her. "That's what I love about this house. It's angled so we have water views from both sides. All the bedrooms overlook the harbor."

He leaned against her. She could feel the heat from his body touching her skin. Memories of his lips caressing hers made her move ever so slightly from him. It wouldn't be great to throw herself in her new boss's arms, begging for another kiss – or something more.

———

Mel cleared her throat. "It's huge, and it could still be an amazing home, if the right people lived here."

She moved to the door. "Well, there's nothing up here. Not a thing. This is very strange, Edward. To have all this destruction and no sign of the cause or its presence in the aftermath. It's very unusual. I can't detect a thing."

He grinned. "Really, and you call yourself a ghostbuster?"

She laughed. "Yep, and proud of it."

"Is this good or bad that you can't sense anything now?"

"Right now, it's good."

"How so?"

"Well it's safe to be in here. We can move from room to room. But the situation is bad because its presence is somewhere else, till it strikes. And that means your mean ghostie is becoming stronger and more powerful."

"Thanks. That makes me feel so much better."

She grinned at Edward. "You asked."

They moved toward the stairs and walked down to the landing. When they reached the foyer, Edward brushed against her arm and once again she felt the warmth of the contact spread through her body.

Mel steeled herself mentally. *Get a grip girl. It's only a touch, for heaven's sake.*

His hand was still on her arm. "Wait a minute. You haven't searched the other side."

"Other side?"

Edward nodded and pointed to the opposite staircase. The other side of my house is a mirror image of the one we just left."

Mel goggled at him. "You mean that there's six more bedrooms on the other side as well? I thought that side must be storage."

He shook his head. "No, that's upstairs. Follow me."

After checking the last bedroom, they walked into the hallway.

"What would they do with all these bedrooms?"

"Well, it was nothing for a family to have ten or more children in the era when this house was built. They had extended families that lived with them too. For example, when the son married he would stay on with his wife and have children. So, the rooms were needed eventually. Archie Ramey just started his family when his wife died in childbirth. He built this home for her as a wedding gift."

"Wow, some wedding gift. Well, the tour was useful. Now I know that the upstairs is free from your mean ghostie."

Edward took her arm. "You're not finished yet, though."

She stared at him. "What do you mean?"

He pointed to the ceiling with his hand. "I mean there's the attic above us."

"The attic?" Mel was beginning to feel as if she was repeating everything Edward said.

She sighed. "Okay, lead the way."

He led her to the end of the hall and opened a large door to another set of twelve steps going up. They weren't as large or as grand as the front stairs, but they were still nice and wide with an oak bannister curving to the landing at the top. As Mel and Edward climbed the stairs, she saw hardwood on the landing above them.

They entered the spacious attic. Closed doors faced each other across a hall that covered the entire length of the mansion.

The first rooms on both sides of the hall were large pleasant bedrooms, just not as large as those downstairs because of the sloped ceilings.

She looked at Edward. "Were these for the staff?"

He nodded. "These front ones were the servants' quarters."

Mel smiled. "I can just detect a presence here. I think it's Katie being very quiet. So, this is likely where she hangs out."

"Is she around now?"

Mel smiled. "She is, but we won't see her."

Edward opened double doors to a room further down the long hall.

"These back rooms are large storage rooms and that's what I've used them for."

She gasped as the door opened wide. "Look at all this lovely antique furniture."

Love seats and ornate mirrors – all circa the Late Victorian era – leaned against ancient chests and tables under the strong ceiling lights.

"They are nice, but they're also reproductions I've had in storage since the movie."

"Really? I don't care if they're not the real thing, I still love them."

They finished investigating the rest of the attic. Each room held well-made reproductions stacked carefully on top of each other.

"Edward, I'm positive about one thing. Whatever is going on in this place, it's not coming from the upstairs. I can't find anything sinister here. Is there a basement in the house?"

He nodded. "There is and it's as large as this attic."

Mel looked at her watch. "I think I'll come back tomorrow and check out the basement."

Edward nodded. "Sounds like a good idea. Why don't we have dinner someplace and you can tell me what you're going to do."

"Alright, and you can tell me where you bought all this wonderful furniture."

They moved across the grand vestibule and stood outside the main entrance. Edward's car was gone. The only vehicle sitting at the curb, was Mel's.

"Looks like Josh needed my car. Can I get a ride back to the B&B with you?"

———

Mel pulled close to the curb at the Mourning Rose. She jumped out and opened the trunk of her SUV to retrieve her bag. Edward took the bag from her hand. She smiled at him. "Thanks, but I can do it."

"Let me take it for you." He grinned. "I don't want you puffing and groaning up the steps again tonight."

She punched him gently on the arm. "You're never going to let me live that one down, are you?"

"No, I'm not."

Her head turned toward the sound of laughter coming from across the street. She glanced over at the couple removing luggage from the trunk of a car.

Mel gasped and felt herself turn to jelly. Luckily, Edward caught her before she hit the pavement.

"Mel, are you okay? What the hell happened, Mel? Mel?" Edward shouted her name again before it sunk in, and all the while waves of shock shook her body.

Panicking, he grabbed her by the shoulders. "Mel? What's the matter? Are you okay?"

She kept shaking her head, trying to pull out of his protective arms. "No. I'm so sorry, Edward. I've just had a horrible shock. Oh my God, Edward, that's David and Liz over there. I can't believe this, but they've come here to Lunenburg on their freaking honeymoon."

He stared at the couple across the street. "Who are David and Liz?"

Mel tried to pull herself together. Her entire body was likely red with embarrassment for the show she'd just put on in front of Edward.

She took a deep breath and calmed herself. "David was the fiancé that dumped me three months ago and Liz was his boss's daughter and one of my bridesmaids. She's, who he dumped me for."

Edward glared across the road at the parked car. "Son of a bitch."

Mel nodded. "I couldn't have said it better myself."

———

A few hours later, Edward and Mel sat back in a secluded corner of an eatery on the waterfront, enjoying a glass of wine after dinner.

She sighed deeply as she watched the moon rising above the gently rocking schooners and smaller boats at anchor in the harbor.

"That was a wonderful meal, Edward. I'm so sorry that I made such a fuss today. I guess I was just surprised that they were here in Lunenburg with us... I mean, where I'm working."

He took her hand. "I would have reacted the same way."

She laughed and shook her head. "No, you wouldn't. You would have gone over and punched him in the nose. I've wanted to do that since he broke off our engagement, but I haven't had the nerve."

Edward took her other hand. "The next time I see him, why don't I go do that for you?"

Mel put her head down and smiled. "Wow, my knight in shining armor. You're su—"

Edward noticed her body stiffen. "They've just arrived, haven't they?"

She nodded, afraid to say anything. Mel could not believe what she was seeing. David and Liz were moving toward their table. She looked up and glued a smile on her face.

David's voice boomed all over the restaurant. "Mel, we heard you were working in Nova Scotia. Fancy meeting you like this."

Liz hung unto David possessively and smiled. "Yes, fancy that."

She could tell David had had a few glasses of wine before arriving at the restaurant. Liz and David stared openly at Edward.

Mel took a deep breath. "Where are my manners? David and Liz Walker, this is Edward White."

Edward stood up and shook Liz's hand and then took David's. Mel smiled with satisfaction when David winced from Edward's handshake.

Mel swallowed hard. "How long are you staying?"

A little tipsy, Liz was obviously uncomfortable as she hung unto David's arm, looking at Mel. "Just two nights, then we're going to do the Cabot Trail in Cape Breton before flying from Halifax to the Bahamas for two weeks on the beach. As you know, Daddy has a villa down there and we're going to use it. Aren't we, honey?"

David nodded, looking at Mel.

Mel pushed the corners of her lips up into what she hoped was a curve. "That's nice. I've read that the best way to view the trail is to do the walking paths and stick as close to the edge as you can."

Liz bobbed her head. "What a good idea. Well, it was nice meeting you, Eddy. Come on honey; let's go back to our room."

David nodded, his gaze never leaving Mel's face. "Nice seeing you, Melly."

She looked him in the eye." It's Mel, David. Only my closet friends and family are allowed to call me Melly...and you, David Walker, are not one of them."

His face reddened with embarrassment. "Why you—?"

Edward sprang out of his chair like a supple big game cat, assessing his prey before pouncing. "I think you'd better leave now. Good night, Mr. Walker."

Liz pulled David away from the table as he looked back. "Come on honey, let's get out of here."

Shaking her head, she watched David leave with his new bride. "I'm glad you did that Edward. I was ready to punch him in the face."

Edward took her hand and laughed. "Oh, I think that

words can cut deeper than knuckles and your words, my girl, cut him to the quick."

Mel laughed. "It felt so good. It's easier when I have a knight in shining armor sitting beside me."

He laughed. "Oh, by the way, walk as close to the edge as you can on the trails'?" He quirked a brow at her. "Really?"

Mel placed her hand over her lips. "I know – wasn't that awful?" She broke into peals of laughter.

"Yes, it was, but they deserved it." Edward chuckled, squeezing her hand.

7

The next morning, Edward used his key to open the door to the Ramey mansion while Mel stood by his side, looking at the exterior of the house.

"Now, let's hope that we can find where that mean ghostie is coming from."

Edward put his key back in his pocket. "The cellar entrance is in the kitchen."

They opened the door to the kitchen and Mel caught movement from the corner of her eye. She looked around and smiled.

"Hi Katie, we're just moving through. We're not here to bother you."

Edward looked back and stared at her. "What did you say?"

"I'm just saying good morning." She followed him to a closed door that led to a large backyard with an amazing view of the harbor.

"What a gorgeous view."

"It's one of my favorite parts of this house and there's a lot I love about this old place."

They looked down the vast expanse of lawn to the water's edge.

"It's so private. I really want to have this for my residence when I'm in Nova Scotia." He turned and touched a light switch at the top of narrow steps.

"This is the entrance to the basement. I think the steps are still okay but be careful. We didn't use this very much for the movie and I haven't had a lot of time or interest to come down here." He chuckled. "This has the original dirt floor. In this area, most of the old homes have cellars instead of basements. Cellars have dirt floors while basements have cement, just so you know."

They entered a large room, roughly twenty feet square with seven-foot ceilings. Two thick wooden doors took up most of one wall. Fragmented light struggled through small, dirty, rectangles of windows above the wooden doors. Bare light bulbs, with frayed cloth cords, hung from the beams holding up the main floor.

Edward moved to where one of the light bulbs dangled from the unfinished ceiling.

"This isn't good. I'm going to have to overhaul all the electrical down here before long."

In the shadowy corners, piles of broken tables, chairs and other furniture that hadn't been moved for at least a century, were just visible in the dim light.

Mel stood on the bottom step. "Wow, this is different from the upstairs."

Edward looked around. "They certainly didn't spend much time or money on the bowels of these houses. After I find out if we're in – or not – with the network, I want to have this cleaned out and restored. That includes better lighting. I'm guessing these walls are the original cut granite."

Mel stepped from the wobbly stairs unto the dirt floor.

"Look at the large doors."

He nodded. "Apparently, Archie used to bring some overflow merchandise from his ships here until his warehouse had room to store them. "Do you want to go further?"

Mel nodded. "I do." She didn't want to mention anything to Edward, but she could feel a presence and the further she moved across the room, the more intense the energy waves were hitting her.

He opened the double door on the far end of room and a long passage way stretched out before them.

He groped for a light switch. "There has to be a switch around here, but I can't find it."

"Edward, there might be a chain dangling from the light."

He moved beneath the light and waved his hand around, trying to locate the chain. "I found it."

Their only beacon of light was dim and very dirty.

Something ran over Mel's foot. She screamed and grabbed Edward's arm.

"What happened?"

"Something ran over my foot. Oh my gosh, I hope that wasn't a rat. I hate rodents of any kind."

Edward chuckled. "You hate rats and yet you go where no one else would go and speak to ghosts... That would have most people running for the hills."

Mel shrugged. "I know. Go figure. I even hate to see a picture of one in a book or on the cover of rat traps."

Edward started to laugh.

Mel was a little upset. "What's so funny?"

"Not a thing, I find you an amazing woman."

Mel snorted. "I'm glad you do. Most men run the other way when they see me coming. That's why I fell so hard for David. He didn't seem to mind that my profession wasn't listed in the catalogues of courses offered by most colleges."

Edward turned and took her in his arms and kissed her firmly on her shocked mouth.

"All I can say is that when he broke your engagement, he missed out on an amazing lifetime journey."

Mel smiled when he let her go.

"Thanks."

"What for? The kiss or the compliment."

Mel whispered. "Both."

A sharp pop from the one hanging light, painted the passageway in darkness again.

Mel gasped. "Oh! Oh!"

"What's wrong, Mel?"

"There's something else about me you should know. I hate the dark."

Edward roared with laughter as he removed his cell phone from his pocket and turned on the phone's light.

Snorting, Mel did the same. "I don't know why we didn't do this before."

"Maybe we enjoyed the ambiance of the place."

She chuckled. "Okay, I'll go along with that."

The phones lit their way, but they could only do and see so much in the long dank corridor.

Two doors, on either side, beckoned them with fingers of long, hanging cobwebs.

"Good grief. I had no idea it was so dirty down here. I thought we had this cleaned up."

She snorted. "I think you should find yourself a new cleaning crew because the one you have now, really sucks." Mel stopped and brushed cobwebs from her face and tried to take some from Edward's back. "Really, really, sucks."

He twisted around. "How are you on spiders?"

"You mean, am I afraid of them?"

He turned around and grinned.

"Nope. I find them charming creatures. How about you?"

Edward paused. "Well, they're not my favorite species on the planet."

She giggled. "Oh, well said." She laughed and kissed his cheek. There, I'll save you from the sweet little spiders and you can protect me from the hateful, disease-filled, disgusting rodents."

Edward roared. "Deal. It sounds like a match made in heaven."

Mel watched Edward laugh and wondered what he'd do if she grabbed him by the collar and planted a huge one on his lips. She sighed. *Focus girl, focus. You're here to detect.*

Suddenly, intense cold encompassed her body.

Edward stopped. "What's wrong?"

"It's here. In this area."

"What is?"

"The nasty spirit that's been wrecking your home."

"You mean it's *here?*" He pointed to the ground and area around him.

"No, I mean this is the area that it's focused on. Its residue is here. We're going to have to turn off our lights and use the thermal scanner to find out if it's still here. She pulled a small box from the pocket of her backpack.

"What does the scanner do?"

"Well it can sense heat. Spirits and every life form give off quite a bit of heat when they move and it's easy to pick them up when it's dark because the heat shows up on the sensors better. If I were to put the scanner up to you, I'd see your outline in the dark as a reddish blue light."

Edward shook his head. "Amazing."

"Yes, it is. I need to go ahead of you." She took a few steps and screamed.

He grabbed her. "What happened?"

Mel gulped. "A rat just scurried away. He came in loud and clear on the scanner."

"You want me to go and beat him up for you?"

Mel shook her head. "Very funny. I don't want you near

that hideous thing. Dim your phone light a little, so I can see more on my sensor."

"I feel as if I'm in training for ghostbusting."

"No, you have to go to school for that."

"There's actual training?"

"You bet, and I'm one of the best teachers you're going to get."

Intense waves of emotion hit Mel's body. She pushed the door on the left side and slowly moved into the room from the almost-dark passage. She felt waves in there too, but they were very weak. She backed out of that room.

Edward backed out of Mel's way, so she could go to the next door.

Before she opened it, Mel knew that she had hit pay dirt. Residual emotions, from previous haunts, filled the dank room with an icy stillness. The stench was pure evil. Mel braced herself against the door frame of what she recognized as a lair from hell.

Edward, close behind her, gasped as the stench seeped into the passageway.

"Cripes, what the hell died in there?"

"Nice, huh?"

She took her scarf and held it up to her nose. It helped a little, but not very much.

"Edward, can you raise your light above me and shine it into the room? I need it on high. I'll keep mine lower to the floor. That way I can see the entire room."

They entered the room together. Edward held the light high above Mel's head, so she could see in every murky corner of the putrid smelling room.

"I've never experienced anything like this before and I hope that I never do again."

Mel snorted. "I guess ghostbusting is not going to be a career change for you, then—"

"This happens all the time for you?"

"Yep, all the time. Can you hold your light a little higher?"

He held the light high above Mel's head as she moved further into the room. She searched every corner.

Suddenly, she shouted: "I knew it."

"What?"

She waved her light into the corner. "Can you point your light in the corner with mine?"

He followed her instructions. "What are we looking for?"

In the corner, on an upturned wooden box with Lunenburg Salt Cod printed in faded blue letters, sat a square board with a rectangular piece of wood on top of it.

"Damn, Edward."

He stared at it. He wasn't sure what he was supposed to be seeing. "What do you mean, the Ouija board? Is that what it is?" Edward moved toward the fish box to get a closer look.

Mel grabbed his arm. "Don't go any further. We don't want to be near that thing yet. I'm just here to observe. How did you know that's a Ouija board?"

"I've known about them since I was a little boy at my grandmother's house."

"Do you know what they *do?*"

Edward looked at her and wondered how much he should tell her.

"I do. They use them to call out to the dead and have a conversation with them."

"That's right. Go to the head of the class."

"Well, this one is set up here and there's no dust on top of it. I'd say that you have a bigger problem than I thought. Someone is calling this spirit out of the depths of evil and beyond."

"What do you mean 'calling' him?"

"I mean that they're using the Ouija board to call this spirit from its world."

"Why the hell would someone do that? And *who* would do that?"

They stood by the door, their lights focused on the one thing that made Mel shake with fear.

"It could be anybody. How many keys were passed around when you started the production of the movie?"

Edward shrugged. "I don't know. I'd have to ask Josh. His team looks after all the mundane. I don't know how many... A lot. There are so many crews that need the keys to the house during filming. One key fits every door. Having it like that was the only way we could get anything done while we were in production."

In the corner, two rats squealed and Mel almost jumped into Edward's arms.

"Let's get out of here. I've had all I can handle in your cellar."

"You don't have to convince me."

He grabbed her hand and almost pulled her out of the room and down the corridor until they reached the large storage room. Still holding her hand at the foot of the basement stairs, he pulled her up the steps so fast that her feet barely touched the treads of the narrow, rickety staircase.

Edward opened the door to the kitchen, pushed the outside door and led her to the deck.

Leaning against the wall of the house they gulped in lungsful of wonderful, sweet salt air.

Mel looked over at Edward. "We need to talk about this."

He nodded, still breathing deeply. "I know a place where we can eat and it's quiet." He took her hand. "It's bad, isn't it Mel?"

She nodded. "I'm afraid so. This puts a whole new slant on what's happening around here."

"What do we do?"

"We find out who's using that Ouija board and why? Then

we wait, Edward. We wait. And we won't say anything about this to anybody."

"Nobody?"

"That's right. Not a word to anybody about what we found. This is very important. We must keep this a secret. I knew there had to be a reason why you've been bombarded by so much activity lately. Someone wants you and your crew to leave and I'm going to find out why. I promise you Edward, I'll get to the bottom of this."

8

Mel waited until the waiter added more hot water to her teapot, then smiled her thanks as he moved away.

Edward grabbed his coffee cup and moved his chair back in the corner where Mel sat, so they could both face the entrance.

He turned to Mel. "Tell me what to do, Mel, and I'll try to do it."

She smiled, looking around. "Thanks for moving to different restaurants, Edward. So far, we've stayed out of David's radar range."

He chuckled. "Was I that obvious?"

Mel smiled. "No, I just know a bit better how you think – and I thank you for that."

He shrugged. "Now tell me what we can do to make this monster go away for good."

She placed her tea cup on the saucer and thought for a moment.

"This is a lot larger than some poltergeist wrecking your set. There's intention behind this."

Edward leaned over the table toward her. "Intention?"

"Yes. There's a reason that the spirit of McGregor has been called to this plane of the universe and that his spirits intense reaction is so tied to something that happened over one hundred years ago."

Edward quirked his eyebrows. "I don't understand."

Mel took a deep breath. It was time for 'Ghostie 101'."

"Well, sometimes you'll get a lot of ghost activity when renovations are being done or if someone died in a home and the specters have not moved on."

"Moved on? You mean to heaven?"

Mel nodded. "Yes, that's right. If they haven't crossed over."

"Crossed over?"

"Yes, to the other side."

She took a sip of her tea. "You see, McGregor never crossed over because there was not an ounce of good in him. So, his essence went to a deeper and darker place."

"I see." He paused. "I think."

"I think you're getting the picture. You're grasping this amazingly well."

"I'm glad you think so."

"You are, Edward, and because he didn't cross over, he can be summoned or pulled back into this plane and when that happens-well you've seen the results."

"So, how does he get here? The Ouija board?"

Mel nodded. "You step to the front of the class."

"But that's not how it is for all spirits...? Like Katie. How come Katie's still here?"

"Ah, that's another reason why we have ghosts. Sometimes they feel an obligation – like Katie does – or they haven't realized that they're dead. Remember Flossie Sarty, the woman I helped cross over when I arrived here? She didn't realize that she had died. Her concern for her little girl was so strong that she kept reliving that moment of the accident for over a hundred years. It was only when I went and helped her realize that she had to move on in order to be with her daughter that she crossed over. Katie, on the other hand, stayed on this side. She could have crossed whenever she wanted to, but she stayed to protect her mistresses."

Edward stared at her. She was waiting for that look that always came when she explained things like this to other guys. But Edward was different from the others. He didn't think her strange at all.

Frustrated, he ran his hand through his hair. "So, I guess the million-dollar question is this: Who summoned McGregor and why?"

Mel nodded. "That's what we have to find out or you're never going to be rid of the destructive force surrounding your house. In fact, with each attack, it's likely to escalate. He's getting stronger because his need for finding whatever he's looking for is becoming more intense."

"And how are we going to do that?"

Mel removed the photocopied journal from her purse and waved it at Edward.

"I think the answer is in Great Annie's journal and we have to find out what it is – and fast."

He quirked his eyebrows. "Her *journal?* Thought you'd been through it before. Why do you say that?"

"Because I think the answer lies in between the lines of what Annie wrote. Remember when I found Katie huddled on the steps and she told me that she wouldn't cross over because she stayed to protect her mistresses?"

Edward nodded his head. "Yes, I remember. I'm still trying to digest that one."

"Well, I asked Katie why McGregor was still here and she said he was looking for something."

"What's he looking for? Did she say?"

"I'm not sure because she was starting to fade when she spoke her last words, but it sounded like...gold."

"*Gold?* Are you sure?"

"No, but it really sounded like it. I'll need to look at any papers with accounts of the time close to the murders."

"I can do that for you. I'll get my staff in L.A. on it right away."

"Oh my gosh, Edward, that would be great. That will save me a lot of time."

She stood up and tucked the journal into her bag. "Now I have to go."

"Where are you going?"

"I need to go back to the house."

"I'll take you."

She faced him and spoke, looking straight into his eyes. With a very firm voice, she shook her head. "No Edward. You are not taking me. I can walk to the house. It's not that far. I need to talk to Katie, if I can find her."

"Cripes, Mel. I'm trying to keep an open mind, but I'm having a very hard time digesting this."

She laughed at the concerned look on his face. "Well, I suggest you buy some Pepto-Bismol for your tummy because you're going to need it."

———

Mel sat at the bottom of the steps on a dining room chair – one that hadn't been broken by McGregor's latest rage. The sun shone through the beautiful stained glass window and she watched dust motes drift in the rays of sunlight filtering in. Taking a deep breath, she summoned Katie with her mind.

"Katie? Katie, can you come and talk to me?"

She waited, but not a sound. This time she spoke out loud...

"Katie, I just want to talk to you. I'm Mel. Remember we spoke before?"

After Mel waited for about five minutes she decided that Katie was not going to come forward. She started to get up when she heard a soft hello. She sat down and waited.

"Hello Katie. Is that you?"

A light swirling mist formed softly around the bottom of the stairs and a translucent Katie emerged, sitting with her hands folded on her aproned lap.

Mel's heart pounded in her chest. It was so exhilarating every time this happened. Speaking to the spirit world never ceased to amaze her. Mentally, she spoke in a light and happy voice.

"Hello Katie. Thank you for coming. Remember me. My name is Mel."

She saw and felt Katie nod.

Mel closed her mind to everything except pulling Katie's voice to her.

Finally, she heard a faint voice. *"Yes, Miss, I do."*

Mel sighed. Wondering how to ask questions of this timid spirit without scaring her away.

"Katie, can you tell me why McGregor keeps coming back?"

Katie took a deep sigh. "He's never left, Miss. He's always been here, bullying us."

"Why is he so mad, Katie?"

"He was looking for sometin', Miss."

Mel tried not to sound too excited. "Something in this house?"

Katie nodded her head.

"Oh yes, Miss. And he wanted it bad. That's all he shouted to us in the kitchen." She paused and her transparent outline faded a little bit.

"When dat terrible ting happened. He kept shoutin', 'Where is it? Where is it?' Oh, it was terrible." Katie started to cry.

Mel knew that what happened a hundred years ago was only yesterday to the little spirit.

The last thing Mel wanted to do was upset this sweet little specter. *"Katie dear, don't cry. He can't hurt you anymore."*

"I stay out of his way, but when those strangers comed in, he went madder and madder, and now he's here all the time. I fear for my mistresses with all my heart. Because that spawn of Satan is so strong. Hast more strength than I have."

Mel was thrilled. Katie's voice was coming through strong and clear.

"What was he looking for?"

Katie started to cry. *"He hurt me, Missus, so bad."*

Mel was afraid that Katie was going to go. *"I'm so sorry, Katie. What was he looking for Katie?"*

"The master's gold and he'll never find it, even if he looks forever."

Mel wanted to reach out and hug the sweet little Irish girl, who was so loyal.

"Katie, don't cry. He can't hurt you anymore."

"He scares me so much, Miss."

Mel sighed. *"I promise you Katie, I'm going to get rid of him."*

The frightened ghost sobbed. *He don't know —sob—that the gold is... Sob, sob."*

Mel could hardly understand what she was saying about the gold.

"Katie, I promise you I will get rid of that monster for you."

Katie's crying was soft and low. *"Oh, Miss, me da always said, don't promise anytin' if your words are going to fly with the wind – and there be a fierce wind blowin' here."* Katie started to fade.

"Katie wait, come back. Please don't go."

Mel watched, frustrated, as the loyal ghost faded away.

She knew that it had taken a lot of energy for Katie to appear to Mel as she had.

"Katie?" Mel leaned into the stairs when she thought she detected a small movement of air, but she sat back disappointed when she realized that it was just the lingering vibes from Katie's visit.

Feeling hopeful she'd return, Mel waited for a few minutes, but Katie had left. Mel stood up and walked toward the door.

She turned around and listened to the stillness of the house. All was quiet and she hoped that it would stay calm for a while.

She opened the door, only to collide with Josh, Dan and Lenny. Mel screamed like a little girl. She heard Josh swear and Lenny hung onto his chest.

Dan grabbed his chest too. "Holy shit, Mel. You scared us half to death."

She started to laugh. "Sorry guys, my heart just had a jump start." She laughed again. "You should see the looks on your faces."

Lenny grinned sheepishly. "Well, ma'am, if your eyes got any bigger, they would have popped right off your face."

"I'm so sorry. I was just talking to Katie and I'm always uptight after a conversation with a spirit."

Lenny's Adam's apple bobbed as he swallowed. "You mean you were talking to a real live ghost, ma'am?"

"I don't know how alive she was, but yes, I was talking to her for a bit."

Josh stared at her. "Well, did you learn anything from her? Please, tell us some good news."

Mel shook her head. "I'm afraid she doesn't have a lot to tell me. She's very timid."

Mel wanted to keep some of the things that Katie had told her to herself and Edward. For now, the rest of the men didn't need to know what Katie had told her about the gold. She needed to find out where the gold was located. It was time to sit down and read the journal again. There must be something in the diary that could help her.

After she said goodbye to the men, she walked down the street wondering what that journal might be hiding. A hand touched her shoulder. She almost jumped out of her shoes. When she looked up, she was ready to throw a punch.

Edward stepped back. "Sorry Mel, I called out to you twice, but your forehead was wrinkled up like you were deep in thought."

She glared at him good-naturedly, and lightly swatted him on his arm.

He laughed. "Oh sorry, I mean you looked pensive."

"Wow, this is the second time I've been scared like that today. My heart must be good."

"Why? What do you mean?"

"Well, I was just opening the door to leave the house and the guys were on the other side ready to enter. We surprised each other on the doorstep and we all screamed like sissies, but don't tell them that I told you I frightened them. It might bruise their egos if you do."

He chuckled. "I promise. Well, did you accomplish your mission?"

She nodded as they walked past the Catholic Church.

"I did."

"You did? You spoke to Katie? Just like we're speaking here?"

"Well almost. I hear her voice, and I feel what she's feeling. Not quite the same..."

She watched those amazing eyebrows rise again and smiled at his confusion. "Uncle Andrew always says, go to the bottom line – so I guess you could say I did talk to her. It wasn't a long conversation, but I found out all I needed to know. I was right. I wish I wasn't because this is certainly going to turn out worse than what it appeared."

Edward tilted his head to one side. "What do you mean?"

"Katie confirmed what I already suspected. McGregor is looking for Archie's gold."

He stopped walking, took her arm and pulled her around so that she was facing him. "Why would a ghost want to know where the gold is, he can't spend it?"

Mel nodded her agreement. "I know, but the person that summoned McGregor, can."

Edward placed his hands on his hips. "Are you telling me that all this destruction and mayhem is because someone is searching for 'a stash of gold'?" He drew quotes in the air with both hands.

"That's what I'm saying."

Edward clenched his fists by his sides. "Son of a bitch."

Mel nodded, looking grim. "My thoughts exactly."

9

M el sat at the Victorian desk in her room with her laptop opened in front of her. Her research about the murders was at a standstill. Her mind should have been on the information in front of her, yet all she could do was look out the window, thinking of how to get rid of McGregor.

Sweet, salty breezes fluttered the lace curtains as she gazed out over the harbor. "Wow, I wonder if the people living here know what a gem they have."

The sound of a couple's laughter drifted up from the street. Mel looked out her window and realized that David and Liz had arrived back at the B&B in their convertible. David helped Liz from the car and then wrapped his arms around her, kissing her long and deeply.

He murmured something and Liz flung her head back and laughed at what he said. They moved out of sight and Mel sat there staring at the laptop screen, unsure how she should be feeling after what she'd just seen.

The theme music for the movie *Ghostbuster* startled her and she grabbed her phone from the desk beside her.

"Mel Gordon, speaking."

"Hi, honey. How's everything going?"

"Hey, Aunt Jo. Well we got a doozy this time. Did you get my report?"

"I did, and I just wanted to see you and talk to you."

"Why?"

"Well I..." Jo paused, hunting for the right words.

Mel sighed. "Let me guess. You heard where David and his bride went on their honeymoon and you're checking on me. Right?"

Aunt Jo grinned sheepishly at her from the screen.

"I did. I just had to know whether you'd seen them, or not."

Mel nodded. "Oh, I've seen them. We saw them at dinner the other night. In fact, I saw them just before you called."

"Oh no, Mel. I'm so sorry. Wait a minute, you said *we*."

"Yes, I did." Mel knew that the short affirmation to the question would be fuel for more of her aunt's questions. "Edward."

"Oh, you were having dinner with him?"

"I did. We have most of our meals together."

"You do?"

"Aunt Jo. Stop it."

Her aunt ignored her, as usual. "What's he like?"

"He's very nice, a true gentleman and he's a wonderful dancer." Mel groaned inwardly. *Oh damn. I've done it now.* The interrogation begins.

"Dancer? You went out dancing?"

Mel laughed. "We did and it was very nice. Now stop it. I mean it, Josephine. I'm okay with David being here. Anyway, he's leaving for the Bahamas, tomorrow."

"How do you know all this?"

Mel sighed again. "We had a very civilized conversation when we met them at dinner and they told us all about their honeymoon plans." Mel's voiced dripped with sarcasm. "Isn't that sweet? They went to the Cape Breton Highlands for a few days and I told them to walk close to the edge of the trails that had a long drop but, Liz didn't quite understand my intent."

Aunt Jo laughed. "Oh, Mel, you didn't. Now they're back? You said that you just saw them?"

Mel nodded at the screen. "Apparently they didn't take my advice." She sighed. "Enough about David and the bride. Today I found out the specter I'm dealing with, is being summoned."

"Summoned? On no. Those are the worst ones. Do you know how and by whom?"

"I think so. I found a Ouija board in the cellar of the house where the destruction has been taking place."

"A Ouija board? Oh, that's bad. Mel, honey, you must be very careful. Every time an evil spirit has been summoned, it becomes stronger. How many other entities are you dealing with?"

"It's hard to tell. One other one for sure, besides Katie, and sometimes I feel two more, but they're not very strong. I've been told that every time it appears, he's stronger than the last time he was summoned. He goes on a rampage because he's looking for something he can't find."

Aunt Jo looked deep into the screen. "*He?*"

"Katie told me his name is McGregor and that he's looking for something."

"Looking for something? What do you think he's looking for?"

"Well, I think that it's gold or something else of great value. It has to be something important for this McGregor to wreck a house and try to injure the people inside."

Aunt Jo interrupted her. "You're sure his name is McGregor?"

"Oh yes, we know who the monster is. And if I can't find his portal and who's calling him, I'm going to need help, Aunt Jo."

"You know, honey, all you have to do is call and we can be there fast. And please don't wait too long. If you think you need us, don't hesitate."

Mel sighed. "I know, Aunt Jo. I don't know how many of the team I'm going to need. But first, I must discover whose summoning him and answer the big question: Why?"

"I know dear. But listen to me. I want you to call as soon as you need us."

Mel laughed at the monitor. "Why? You're going to know before I do anyway."

Jo laughed. "I know, but this is your case and we can't come barging in until you call us. Promise me that you will and that you won't try to do this on your own."

"Okay. Okay I promise. I'd rather have help with this one anyway. If I think that it's too much for me, I'll call you...both ways. I promise."

"Now I feel better. Goodbye, dear. Love you."

Mel threw a kiss at the screen. "Love you too."

She broke the connection and sat looking at her blank screen for several minutes, trying to understand and piece together the arrival of McGregor with some of the questions that she and Aunt Jo had just gone over. But she was still in the dark about how to find out who was behind the summons of the horrible specter.

Mel reopened her e-mail to check information about the murders that had been sent to her. Her phone rang.

"Mel Gordon speaking."

"Mel, this is Edward."

Her stomach did a little flutter. *Wow. What's all that about?*

"Hi, Edward."

"Mel, I'm going to be a little late for dinner. I'm over here at the house with the guys, walking through the sets. I'll pick you up in ten minutes."

"You don't have to pick me up. I'll just walk over to meet you."

"Are you sure?"

"Of course. Any excuse to walk the streets of Lunenburg."

He laughed and Mel smiled. He had a wonderful laugh. It sounded good.

"That's great, Mel. I'll make a Lunenburger out of you yet."

"Too late, Edward. I'm already smitten."

There was a pause. "I hope it's with more than the town, Mel."

She caught her breath. *Wow, wow, wow*. She laughed, hoping he couldn't tell how shaky she was and how much that question affected her.

"Let's say that Lunenburg has become very special to me. See you in ten minutes."

Mel left her room and ran down the steps until she reached the landing of the reception area. There, she slowed to a dignified walk, said hello to Alice at reception and smiled hello to the charming ghost couple that passed in front of her before she reached the sidewalk.

Mel's light mood fell into a dark crevice when she looked across the street and saw David standing by his car, watching her walk down the steps.

He waved as he wove toward her.

"Oh great," Mel mumbled, "He's drinking." She took a deep breath. "This is all I need."

She pretended that she hadn't seen him and walked down the sidewalk.

David caught up with her. "Melly, wait up."

She turned and faced him. "I'm really in a hurry, David. I have to meet Edward in five minutes."

He stood in front of her, swaying a little. "Too busy to stop and talk to your fiancé?"

She looked him straight in the eye. "Ex fiancé to you. And yes, I'm too busy. Goodbye David." She walked down the street.

He shouted. "But, I want to talk to you."

She turned, with her hands on her hips. "Well, I don't want to talk to you. I have nothing to say. Go back to your little bride, David."

She turned the corner and looked back. David just stood there, staring after her.

A golden retriever ran from her Victorian-styled dog house. The name Willow was painted above the entrance. The beautiful dog ran to the white, wrought iron, ornate fence of the property and stood there wagging her tail at Mel.

She stopped and patted its head.

"Hello Willow. I didn't see you the last time I went for a walk. You want some advice, girl? Be careful who you date, or you might make a big mistake like I did. See this smile, Willow? I'm so happy, and a few months ago I got jilted by the biggest jerk around."

Willow's tail banged constantly against the fence and it seemed she nodded her head in agreement with everything Mel said. Her long tongue licked Mel's hand in sloppy dog kisses.

Mel turned another corner and walked up one last steep hill to the house.

Edward walked down the steps to the sidewalk to greet her. His smile gave her heart little flip flops.

She stood still, trying to catch her breath. "Man, that last hill is a doozy."

Josh, Dan and Lenny came through the door and Josh locked it behind them.

Dan waved. "Hey Mel, I hear you're going for lobster."

She grinned at them. "I am? Again?"

Edward turned around and laughed at Dan. "That was supposed to be a surprise."

Dan laughed. "Sorry, I didn't know."

"That's okay, Dan, unless Edward was going to blindfold me I would have realized it once he started driving anyway." Mel was still short of breath from Edward's greeting.

Edward took her by the arm. "It's such a nice night. I thought we'd walk to dinner."

Her heart dropped. She was pooped. Still, she put on a brave face.

"That sounds great, Edward." She saw him wink at the guys and laughed, realizing he'd been teasing her. "Oh, thank goodness. If I had to walk one more hill tonight, I'd fall flat on my face."

They all laughed as Edward took her arm and opened the car door for her.

She waved above the windshield at the guys standing on the sidewalk, grinning. "See ya guys."

Lenny waved. "Have a nice time, Ma'am."

Mel shook her finger at him. "Lenny, will you stop calling me ma'am. Call me Mel."

His face turned red. "Yes, Ma'am, uh... I mean Mel."

Edward's reserved table overlooked the water and the lush greenery of the Lunenburg Golf Course.

After a delicious lobster dinner, he pushed his plate aside and took out his notebook. "I've had my office do some research and they found out something very interesting."

His phone rang and he pulled it out of his pocket, looked at it and shook his head. Instead of answering, he took Mel's hand and held it.

"I'll take it later. I just want to spend some down time with the most attractive Ghostbuster I've ever seen."

Mel laughed and this time kept her hand in his. She gazed

into his eyes and smiled. "How many ghostbusters do you know?"

He chuckled. "Well, those four guys from the movie."

She pulled her hand from his and swatted him gently on the arm.

"Well, thanks a lot. I could look like a dog and still look better than they did."

Edward chuckled. "Trust me Mel, you do not look like a dog unless, it was an exceptionally pretty and intelligent dog."

He looked at his watch. "I'm afraid it's time to go back to the B&B. I have an early morning tomorrow. I need to be at the airport to pick up electrical equipment that's being flown in by UPS."

————

At the Mourning Rose, they said goodnight to the receptionist and climbed the stairs together.

Mel took her key out and unlocked her door. Edward stood close behind her. She turned to say good night, but before she could utter the words, he took her in his arms and kissed her deeply.

"I had a very nice time tonight, Mel." He kissed her once more. "A very, very, nice time."

She smiled. "So, did I, Edward. Goodnight and have a safe trip." Then, surprising herself, she placed her arms around his neck and kissed him back.

"Thank you for a lovely dinner."

The kiss vibrated deliciously through her body. Startled, she pulled away and they both began to laugh, as once again his phone vibrated between them. They clung to each other, giggling.

"I'm sorry, Mel. This is not a very good way to end such a nice evening."

She laughed and hugged him. "Oh, I wouldn't say that."

He stepped aside and answered his phone. "Hi Josh. What? Oh, wait a minute." He rooted around in his pocket, then produced a key.

"Yeah, I have it. I'll drop it off now because I need to be at the airport at five tomorrow morning."

She waved, as she opened the door. "Goodnight, Edward."

He smiled as he moved toward the stairs. "Night Mel. See you tomorrow."

She shut the door and leaned against it. The kiss had been amazing, even without the vibrating phone.

She ran her bath and eased her tired body into the fragrant water of the amazing tub. Looking through the low window, she could see the moon shining its light, like a beacon on the water above the Battery.

Later, she sat in front of the laptop and read the information sent to her about a robbery.

She was so deep into the research, she barely heard the knocking at the door. The second knock was louder and she jumped up to answer it, knowing it was Edward.

She opened the door wide and came face to face with David, drunk as a skunk.

"David, what the hell are you doing here? How did you get past reception? Please leave. Right now."

David stood in the doorway swaying. "Melly, baby, I made a mistake. I've decided that you're coming back to me."

Mel snorted. "When pigs fly. Go away, David, before I scream. Why would I ever want to go back to you? You're married and on your honeymoon. You stupid jerk. It was the best thing you ever did for me, when you left me for Liz."

Tears ran down his face. "I was wrong."

He swayed and leaned in. Grabbed her by the arms. Tried to kiss her.

Mel struggled out of his grasp. "Get your dirty hands off me, you asshole. Now leave."

He puckered his lips, trying to zero in on her face. "No, I'm not. You're mine."

He leaned in closer to kiss her while she struggled to get out of his arms.

"David, I'm telling you one more time. Get out of here."

"No. You're mine and I want you. You're *messsshhh-ing* around with Mr. Producer and I want s-s-s-ome of the action he's getting."

He slurred the words right in her face. "Checked him out. He's loaded. That why

you won't come back? You still belong to me."

He leaned closer. "I want some action."

She glared daggers at him. "You want some action? Here it is."

Mel grabbed his shoulders. David who'd been thinking that Mel was coming around to his way of thinking, leaned in for a kiss. She raised her knee high, aiming for David's groin. She heard the wind leave his lungs and felt elation, knowing that her knee had hit her target – right on.

———

Edward muttered an oath as he reached the top of the stairs. He reached Mel's door just in time to see David collapse, moaning.

Edward pulled him up to a standing position and pushed David against the wall.

"David, can you hear me?" he asked.

David nodded, his eyes glassy from pain.

"Okay, listen very carefully. If I ever catch you anywhere near Mel again, I'm going to hurt you really bad. Do you understand?"

David's face had lost all color with the injury Mel had given him. He grew even paler.

Edward half dragged, half carried him to the stairs. "Now you get your sorry carcass out of here, before I finish what Mel started."

Grabbing him by the shoulders, Edward stared into his eyes. "This is not a friendly warning, David. Do you understand?"

David nodded and leaned on the oak bannister for support. He moaned in pain then stumbled down the steps, glaring at Mel through the rungs of the banister. "You bitch," he told her.

Edward moved toward him, but Mel grabbed his arm. "Let him go, Edward. His bark is worse than his bite."

Edward grinned. "Right now, it is. Are you okay?"

She nodded and smiled. "Oh, I'm fine."

He grinned. "What the hell did you do to him?"

"I kneed him."

Edward roared with laughter. "You certainly did. I think that he's going to have a very neglected bride in the Bahamas."

She grinned. "I hope so."

"Remind me not to get on your bad side."

She smiled. "Oh, I don't think that's going to be a problem, unless you ask me to marry you and then leave me for one of my bridesmaids."

She stood inside the door, with it opened in invitation, but he remained outside, looking in.

"Goodnight again, Edward. Safe trip to the airport."

"Thanks, Mel. Goodnight."

He stood smiling at her back as she turned and entered her room. He walked across the hall, turned to gaze at her closed door and chuckled.

"Oh, Mel, Grandmother's going to love you."

10

Mel groped for the phone on the side table by her bed. She squinted at the clock. Seven fifteen.

"Who the hell...?" She tried to clear her throat.

"Hello? Mel Gordon, speaking."

Josh's voice screamed in her ear: "Mel, for cripes sake, get down here right now. I called Edward and he's on his way home from the airport. Hurry."

Josh broke off the connection. Mel threw her clothes on as fast as she could and within five minutes was turning into the cul-de-sac that was already filled with flashing lights.

She jumped out of the Jeep and met Dan on the front steps. Tears were running down his cheeks.

"Dan? Tell me what happened? What's wrong, Dan?"

He wiped his eyes with the back of his hands. "It's bad, Mel. It's really bad."

She grabbed his arms. "What is? Tell me."

"It's Lenny. Oh my God, Mel. It's Lenny."

"Lenny? What happened? Tell me."

"I don't know. He's not moving. The paramedics are in there now, but he's just lying there in a heap."

Josh ran from the house and joined them. "Oh, thank God – here's Edward."

Edward pulled in behind a first responder's vehicle with flashing lights. He wasted no time and sprinted up the formal steps, three at a time. Josh grabbed him. "Thank God, you're here."

"What the hell happened?"

Dan wiped his tear-stained face with the back of his hand. "I don't know, we went in this morning to check on props and to make sure that the lighting angles were going to be right. We were all over the place. I was in the kitchen when I heard Lenny scream. I ran from the kitchen and passed the dining room. That's where I saw Lenny hanging about three feet above the floor like someone was holding him up by his collar. I swear on my mother's grave, it looked like a dark shadow of a man."

Josh's face was glistening with sweat. "Cripes Edward, it looked more like a giant. A black giant."

Dan wrung his hands. "And then whatever that thing is, it tipped its head back and let out the same horrible scream that we heard before." He looked apologetically at Mel.

"I wanted to help, but I couldn't move. I was so terrified. And then..." Dan paused and swiped at the tears that flowed from his eyes. He took a deep breath, then continued. "And that thing just held Lenny up, shook him like a rag doll, roared that horrible laughter so loud that the windows vibrated. Then it threw Lenny down the stairs. He flew over some steps and bounced on others before he hit the marble floor with a horrible thud, sliding in his own blood until he lay there like a pile of old rags. I'll never forget the sound of that thud."

Edward and Mel just stared at Dan, shell shocked.

Mel couldn't believe the amount of blood on the floor. "Oh my God, how is he?"

Dan shook his head. "I don't know. Josh was in there, but they wouldn't let him near Lenny." More tears flowed. "I think he's dead, Edward. I think Lenny's dead."

Josh nodded. "I tried to find out what was going on, but they kicked me out."

The door opened and a fireman asked them to stand back. Two paramedics carried Lenny out on a gurney. The fireman ran in front of the paramedics and opened the back of the ambulance for them.

Edward sucked in air at the sight of Lenny, the gentle man, lying there unmoving. Lenny's face was partially covered with an oxygen mask and his left leg was out at a forty-five-degree angle. A concerned fireman, running alongside the gurney, held the mask steady over Lenny's face.

Edward stood beside the ambulance, watching as they pushed Lenny's gurney between the open double doors of the ambulance.

———

They sat in the emergency room of Fishermen's Memorial Hospital for what seemed like hours and waited for a doctor or anybody to come out and tell them anything. They prayed it wouldn't be what they were terrified to hear.

Edward stood up, pulled his hand through his hair. "I can't handle much more of this."

He walked to the nurse's station and a nurse, whose name tag read Geraldine Daniels, looked up and shook her head.

"I'm sorry, Mr. White. I still haven't heard anything from inside." She looked down at her computer and then at the double closed doors at the end of the corridor. As a kind gesture, the nurse placed her hand over Edward's and looked compassionately to where the others sat, stunned and scared, huddled together for support.

She watched their strained faces. "We'll hear something soon, I promise. Dr. David Emeneau is the best in his field."

The double doors, where Lenny had been rushed through, opened and everyone stared as a distinguished-looking man in his early sixties walked toward them. He grabbed a chair from the corner and brought it over and sat in front of them.

"I'm Dr. David Emeneau." He leaned forward and clasped his hands between his legs, took a deep breath and shook his head. "I'm not going to beat around the bush. He's in rough shape and it's not good."

He watched different emotions flit across the faces of the people in front of him.

"Mr. Walt has been prepped for Halifax and he's going to be airlifted to the QEII. We're just waiting for the Medevac Flight to land. Surgery is on standby and as soon as they touch down in Halifax, he'll be rushed to the operating room."

Mel watched as Dr. Emeneau stared at each face, in turn.

"That must have been some fall. We almost lost him once inside."

She watched as he stared at all of them. His tired, but intelligent brown eyes, looking and waiting for more details. *How could you tell a man of science that a ghost attacked his patient?* That wouldn't go over big.

She cleared her throat. "Lenny fell down a lot of stairs and landed hard on a marble floor."

Dr. Emeneau nodded, still watching her. "Well, that explains a lot. He has a concussion and multiple broken ribs. One rib punctured his right lung. At this point, we can't be sure what other damage the ribs have done. We've tried to stabilize him. Right now, he's in a coma. That's all we can do here. Let's hope it's enough."

Josh jumped up. "I'll go with him."

Dr. Emeneau raised his hand. "It's not going to do you or Lenny any good. He's going to surgery as soon as he arrives at the hospital."

He pulled out a paper pad from his pocket and wrote down a few scribbled words, tore the page off and passed it to Edward. "This is the hospital liaison's name and number at the hospital for the family of patients going through surgery. I've already given their team your name, so whenever you call they'll tell you exactly what's taking place. You can call day or night."

Josh stood up. "Can we go in and see him?"

Dr. Emeneau shook his head. "Son, that's the last thing you want to do. You're not going to know what's going on until they perform surgery. So, stay here in Lunenburg. Let the surgeons do their work. Lenny will have some of the best in the world working on him in Halifax."

Dan sat on a blue plastic chair with his head down and his knuckles white from clenching. "What... What are his chances, Doc?"

The doctor placed his hands on his knees and looked at all of them, staring at him, waiting for his answer.

He sighed. "I'm not going to give you any false hope. It's serious. Because of all the damage to the lungs and the ribs, there's internal bleeding. We can't be sure what other organs are involved. If he makes it through surgery – and I mean *if* – he might have a fighting chance. His family should be notified right away and..."

He stared at Mel. "And don't paint a pretty picture for them, because it isn't. Prepare them, so the shock won't be so bad if he doesn't pull through."

A deep sob escaped Dan's throat. "He doesn't have any family. The company is the only family he has."

Edward looked at the doctor. "Oh my God. I feel so help-less. What can I do?"

Dr. Emeneau rose wearily from his chair and placed a hand on Edward's shoulder.

"Pray. The surgeons are going to need all the help they can get."

Dan sat up. "Lenny always said it was easy for him to travel all over the place because of no family. He used to come home with me when we were stateside."

The roar of the helicopter settled over the hospital and they ran out to the side windows and watched the huge bird hover over the ground before landing.

The doctor rushed down the corridor and disappeared through the double doors.

Mel and the others stood frozen, by the large hospital windows, watching. Bent close to Lenny's body, a team of doctors and nurses, led by Dr. Emeneau, pushed his gurney to the side of the helicopter. Paramedics jumped out and assisted in lifting him into the big bird. The paramedics gave them the thumbs-up sign.

Dr. Emeneau and his team backed away. The doors shut, removing Lenny from sight. The copter rose into the air amid the swirling debris of the parking lot, circled once and angled its nose toward Halifax.

They stood and watched. Mel whispered a prayer as tears ran down her cheeks. "Please, dear God. Please make that sweet gentle man better."

A pulse throbbed at the corner of Edward's jaw. "Okay, let's go." Mel touched his arm. "Go where?"

"We're going back to the Mourning Rose. We need to have a meeting. We can't do anything more here now. When he recovers, he's going to need us."

Josh mumbled. "If, he recovers."

Edward shook his head at Josh. "No, we have to think

positive, and for now we must decide what we're going to do. I know what I have to do. I'm canceling the show."

———

They filed into the Mourning Rose's dining room. The staff had placed three tables together. Outside on the closed, double French doors a sign read: Closed until six pm.

Amy, their waitress, brought pots of tea and coffee to fill their cups. She placed large trays of sandwiches and fruit on the table, then stood in front of Edward's chair.

"Anything else, Mr. White?"

He shook his head. "No that's fine, Amy. We appreciate it very much."

She smiled. "I'll just check and see how you're doing in a little while. I promise you no one will bother you."

Mel watched the couple in the corner look over and smiled at her. *Still happy, still smiling and still very dead.*

Edward took a long drink of his coffee. "Now, what the hell happened?"

Josh and Dan looked at each other and shrugged their shoulders.

Josh took a sip of his hot coffee and poured some more. "Well, you know we were going over early to size up the main floor for the lighting and sound. I went to the kitchen."

Dan nodded. "And I was in the foyer, but went to the kitchen to pick up notes I'd left on the table. Lenny, went upstairs to see how much line we'd have to split. It took a while because Lenny and I were talking back and forth on our phones.

"We heard Lenny scream and then this roar filled the whole damn house. Like we told you before, I hollered to Lenny because it sounded like he had fallen off a ladder. I heard another crash like the ladder fell over." Dan swallowed hard. "Josh and I ran from the kitchen to see that shadow holding Lenny at least three feet above the floor. Then it tossed Lenny and he came flying down the steps. He hit the other steps just below the window and then..."

He looked over at Edward. "I swear to God, Edward, it looked like someone picked him up and threw him again. He flew down the next flight of steps, hitting some on his way and then he landed, sprawled on the marble floor about six feet away from the staircase."

Josh was nodding his head. "That's right, we heard this blood-curdling scream from that thing. Lenny just lay there, lifeless."

Dan swallowed hard, trying to keep his composure. He pressed his lips together. "His... His body slid in his own blood on the marble floor. He lay all crumbled up in a heap, without moving. Man, I never saw anything like it."

Josh took a deep breath. "I called 911 and then I called you and Mel. All the while, this monster was on the rampage above us. The doors slamming so hard, I'd be surprised if they're still on their hinges."

Mel and Edward sat there, dumbfounded.

Edward took a gulp of coffee. "So, what's been damaged?"

Josh shrugged. I don't know. I wanted to go in and assess the damage, but to be honest with you, I'm afraid."

Dan looked down at his coffee. "That goes for me, too."

Mel shook her head. "It's, okay, guys. What you saw happen to poor Lenny is not the usual and I can promise you that you won't be bothered by him again today. McGregor is not going to do anything more now. He's tapped out all his anger and energy. He'll have to recharge before he can go on another rampage like this last one. I'll come with you. I want to go inside and see if I can detect anything."

Edward glared at her. "There is no way in hell that you're

going to go back in there with that thing roaming around. It's not necessary. I told you, I'm canceling the series."

Mel sighed. "Edward, I'm going to make sure that he's dealt with before he can do it again and then you can get your show on the ground and running."

"I told you, I'm canceling it."

Mel shook her head. "You can't cancel it. When Lenny leaves the hospital, do you want him to shoulder the guilt that it was because of him that the show was canceled? That's not fair to him."

She looked at Josh and Dan. "I think we should vote on it. All those in favor of continuing to prepare for the show, raise your hand."

Mel's hand shot up. She looked at Josh and Dan. Hesitantly, they both raised their hands. Edward kept his on the table. She smiled at him. "I guess you got your answer."

"So, how will this play out, Mel? This can't go on."

"Edward, you've got something happening here that I've never encountered before. I'm calling in reinforcements. My Aunt Jo is in the same field that I am and between the two of us..."

Edward interrupted her. "There is no way in hell I'm going to let you go near that place. I'll shut it down and then I'll burn it to the ground first."

Mel shook her head. "Edward, let me do this. This is my job. And you're not burning the lovely old house down. Not now. Not ever."

She drank the last of her tea. "Let's go to the house. We'll all go in and assess the damage."

———

They entered the house. Lenny's blood still smeared the

stairs. Some of it had also dried on the marble floor in the foyer.

They stood inside the door, not really wanting to go any further.

Dan covered his mouth. "Man, what *is* that smell?"

Josh gagged. "Jeese, it smells as if a sewer backed up a hundred years ago, in a molasses factory."

Edward placed an arm over his nose and mouth. "God, that's awful."

Mel walked to the middle of the room, closed her eyes and took a deep breath. Turning a few times she opened her eyes and looked over at the men, huddled close to the door, watching her.

She smiled. "He's gone. His presence is gone. She sniffed the air. "Yuck, his smell lingers on."

No one argued. The room smelled as though someone had mixed manure, brimstone and molasses.

Mel waved her hand in front of her face. "It's still here because it was so intense. Open the doors and let some of the stink out."

Josh and Dan both took a deep breath and went up the stairs. Dan led the way and shouted: "Holy shit, Edward. You should see what the son of a bitch did up here."

They followed them up the stairs. The destruction, as they entered the second story, took Mel's breath away.

They looked around incredulously. Every door was off its hinges, with some half-lying on the floor or propelled deep into the plastered walls. Other pieces of the doors and frames, smashed so bad they resembled kindling, were strewn everywhere over the hall's wide hardwood floor.

Edward gasped. "Oh my God. What the hell happened here?"

He looked at Mel. "Are you telling me one ghost did all this?"

Mel nodded. "It did."

He stared at the destruction then looked at her in shock.

"*Why*, in heaven's name?"

Mel shrugged her shoulders. "I don't know. This thing is being coached and egged on to do this by someone. Whatever this ghost was when he was alive, he is worse now. Someone has him all fired up."

Edward ran his hands through his hair. "Mel, what do I do?"

She stepped over broken doors and chairs, pushed some abused furniture aside and sat down on the top step of the stairs.

Mel shook her head. "I've never seen or heard of so much energy radiating from one spirit. Someone strongly motivated to cause harm is behind this, Edward. Someone that doesn't care who or what they hurt."

He sighed. "Why? Why would they do this?"

She shook her head. "Edward, when living people are mean, that personality doesn't change when they die. They're unable to pass over because they don't deserve to see the light. That means we're dealing with something very evil — malevolent beyond what we can imagine."

He sat down beside her on the top of the stairs. Mel squeezed over. Their shoulders rubbed against each other and she felt the reassuring heat from his body warm hers. She took his hand and held it.

"Don't worry, we'll get to the bottom of this and then resolve it."

He sighed, his voice thick with emotion. "I don't care about any of this, Mel. This can all be repaired or replaced. It's Lenny, I'm sick with worry about. They should have called by now."

He looked at his watch. "It's six hours since they took him away."

She squeezed his hand. "Well, that's a good thing. It means he's still in surgery. That's good, isn't it?"

"Yes, I guess so, but waiting isn't one of my strong points." He stood up and looked down at her.

"So, I'm going to go to Halifax and see what's going on for myself."

Mel smiled, in sympathy. "You know that means sitting in the waiting room until someone has the time to see you. It could be hours..."

"I know that. I don't care if I have to sit there for three days. I'm going to be there in case Lenny needs me."

Mel stood up. "Okay, let's go."

He squeezed her hand.

"Thanks, Mel. I really appreciate that you would offer to come with me. Are you sure you want to come along?"

Mel looked around at all the destruction.

"I can't do anything here until after the vibes settle down. And it should be cleaned up. That room downstairs was McGregor's point of entry. I know if I can find his specific portal down in your cellar, then I can block it and send him back to where he came from."

Edward stared at her. "You mean hell, don't you?"

Mel stepped over a piece of door that had been thrown halfway down the stairs. She looked around.

"Well, he didn't come from heaven."

"I think, Mel Gordon, that's the understatement of the year."

11

The traffic was very light. They arrived at the hospital in less than an hour. Once inside the doors, they moved to the information desk.

Edward pulled his phone from his pocket, checking the name that Dr. Emeneau had given him.

An attractive brunette, in her early thirties, wearing a happy face nametag with Cathy on it, smiled. "Can I help you?"

Edward nodded. "Hi, our friend, Lenny Walt, is here having surgery and we were told to contact Brenda Conrad as soon as we arrived."

Checking the ledger, she nodded. "Go to the first set of elevators." She pointed to their left. "Stop at the tenth floor, turn right and ask at the desk for Brenda. I'll call up and tell them you're coming up."

When they entered the elevator, a little lady wearing a hot pink flowered housecoat followed behind them. Edward held the doors open so she could enter. She smiled her thanks and he returned the smile.

The elevator doors opened at the tenth and they all

moved into the corridor. The little lady smiled again and turned a corner.

"Cathy gave great directions." Edward looked around. "Wow, that woman sure can move for a little old lady."

Mel's head snapped in Edward's direction. "You saw her in the elevator?"

He raised his eyebrows. "Yes, why? I'm not blind. She looked very nice."

Mel smiled, shaking her head. Good grief. *She looked very nice*. Now, that was one she hadn't heard before.

They moved toward the desk. A lovely woman, in her mid-fifties with short black hair flecked with gray, walked toward them dressed in surgery scrubs. Extending her hand to Edward, she smiled.

She shook Mel's hand too. "Hi, I'm Brenda. I'll take you to the family room and get you settled. The cafeteria is on the main level of the east tower. If you're not in the waiting room when I come to make a report, I'll just call you to come up."

Edward smiled his thanks. "Can you tell us anything about Lenny?"

Glancing at her clipboard, she shook her head. "Not yet. As soon as I hear anything, I'll let you know." She smiled sympathetically at their concern. "I promise."

She led them through a door with a sign at eye level that read: For Family Only. Calm and soothing, the room was filled with earth-colored reclining chairs. Muted news projected from a large flat-screen television hung on the wall. By the window, a metal table with wheels, held thermoses with coffee and tea and an assortment of snacks.

When Edward sat down and removed his phone, Mel sauntered over and sat next to him.

"Edward. Did you really see that lady in the elevator?"

Edward, with his head down, looking at his phone, nodded. "I did, why?"

"Well, I saw her very clearly, but because I have a gift. You see, I have been trained and that's what I do for a living."

His head snapped up. "What do you mean?"

"Well," Mel sighed. "I saw her because she's a ghost and you saw her... *Why?*"

Edward grinned. "I did see her, but I didn't realize she was a ghost."

"So, did you see that couple at our B&B?"

He nodded. "I did. They're very nice, aren't they?"

She smiled. "They are Edward. And they're dead. They've been dead for over one hundred years."

"What? You're kidding? You are saying I see and sometimes talk to ghosts? No wonder when I speak to some people, they just move away like I didn't exist."

"How long have you been seeing dead people?" she asked.

"I don't know. Maybe it goes back to when my grandfather passed away. His funeral was in the morning and I was sitting on the swing, in his backyard that same evening – the one that he built for me. I loved my granddad so much. I was crying hard and the swing moved. I looked up and there he was smiling down at me, all shiny and bright. He looked so good."

"In the year before he died, he had developed cancer and by his death it had eaten away at the him until he was just a shell of the man he used to be. That night, it was like the cancer had never been. He bent over and asked me if I wanted a push. He patted me on the arm. I can still feel his touch. I could smell his Old Spice aftershave. Every time I smell that, I think of Gramps. He was a very special man. So is my gram." He looked around then asked, "Can I get you anything to eat?"

"No thanks. Weren't you afraid when you saw your grandfather? Some people are, you know."

He snorted. "Afraid? Far from it. Not when Granddad told me that he was happy and in a better place. Are you sure you don't want to go to the cafeteria?"

She shook her head. "I'll just have a doughnut and some tea here. I want to look at the journal again and see if I've missed any clues about what is going on at your place."

Edward ran his hands through his hair. "Anything at all would be a godsend."

"I know and I have this nagging feeling time is running out."

The waiting game began.

From time to time, Brenda would pop her head in and shake her head. "Nothing, yet. How are you doing?"

They'd both nod. She'd wave and leave the room.

Hours passed.

Brenda came in again and sat down beside them. She stared at her clipboard.

Mel swallowed. Brenda didn't make eye contact. This didn't look good. It didn't look good at all.

"Okay, here it is. Lenny's finally left surgery and is back in ICU. It's too early to tell anything. He survived the ordeal of surgery, but only time will tell. His ribs did a lot of damage to the lungs, and some of his organs are very bruised. We're putting him in an induced coma, so there's less stress on his body until he starts to heal. We're waiting to see if he can breathe on his own, after he wakes from surgery, before we induce the coma. That's a major test Lenny has to pass. If he's not able to breath on his own…" She paused and shrugged.

Edward took Mel's hand.

Brenda leaned over and placed her hands on their knees.

"Listen to me. He's tough. Against all odds, Lenny survived surgery. No one thought he would. That's a huge step in the right direction."

Edward nodded and sighed. "Can we see him?"

Mel swiped away her tears with the palm of her hand.

Brenda sighed, shaking her head.

"No. Go home. You're as close as the phone. You carry yours with you, Edward?"

He patted his pocket. "Right here. And I can be back in forty minutes."

"You're in Lunenburg, right?" They nodded. "I think I'd like you to drive instead of fly." She smiled. "I don't want to have to be checking on you after an accident. Take an hour to get here, okay?"

He smiled. "Okay."

"Good. As soon as I have any news, I'll call you – day or night. I promise."

She stood up and looked down at them. "Now, go home and try to carry on with your normal lives. Look after yourselves. Lenny is getting the best care we can give him."

Walking to the car and climbing in, they hardly spoke, each wrapped up in their own thoughts. Mel took Edward's hand and held it. Edward stroked her hand with his thumb. Ten miles from the Lunenburg ramp, Edward's phone rang. He looked at it. "It's Brenda."

Mel held her breath as Edward turned on his Bluetooth and answered the phone so she could hear.

He cleared his throat. "Hello."

"Edward, this is Brenda, Lenny has..." Her voice faded out on the phone.

He paled and Mel gasped, threw her hands on her face and moaned. "Oh, dear God."

Brenda's voice came in loud and clear. "Edward, can you hear me?"

"Yes, Brenda. We can now. We must have hit a dead spot. Is Lenny...? Is he—?"

"It's good news, Lenny started breathing on his own. He's not out of danger yet, but that's a very positive start. Thought you should know."

"Thank you, Brenda. Thank you so much."

"You're welcome. Hope this makes your day better. I'll keep in touch."

Tears of relief ran down Mel's face. The more she tried to stop them, the harder they flowed. Sobbing, she looked at Edward. "I thought... I thought she said...that he had died."

He pulled over on the side of the road. Embracing Mel with his arms, he kissed the top of her head."

"I know Mel. I know. I thought the same thing."

He held her until her sobs subsided into little hiccups.

She tried to pull away, but he kept his arms wrapped gently around her.

"I'm okay now, Edward. I'm so sorry, this is not a very professional way for a ghostbuster to act."

Edward lowered his head and kissed her.

Mel closed her eyes and wrapped herself in the warmth of his arms.

Ending the kiss, he looked into her eyes. "Oh, Mel." He kissed her again, deeply.

A passing car, tooted. They both laughed and Edward sat back on his side of the car. "Now, that was the best celebration kiss I ever had with a ghostbuster."

She laughed. "Hope that was the only kiss you ever had with a ghostbuster. The only other one I know is Aunt Jo and I'm not sure she'd appreciate the kiss." She paused and smiled. "As much as I did."

He roared with laughter. "Let's go back and tell the guys the great news about Lenny, in person."

———

Hand in hand, they walked to the third floor. At her door, Edward took her in his arms and kissed Mel again.

She hung on to this man, who she now realized, she loved so much. Mel left his embrace, turned and opened her door wide. She smiled at him.

"Stay with me, tonight."

"Are you sure, Mel?" He moved closer and took her hand, watching her face intently.

She squeezed his hand and laughed, her heart full of joy. "Oh, Edward, I've never been so sure of anything in my life."

Pulling her into his arms, he kissed her passionately and closed the door behind them.

12

The next morning when Mel woke, Edward was gone. She stretched and smiled at her memories from the night before.

"Get up lazybones. They're waiting for you at the house," she told herself.

Heavy fog was still hanging in the air when she stepped onto the sidewalk. The sun hadn't had time to burn it off, and in the distance a fog horn sounded mournfully.

Mel wanted to go to Edward's house by herself. Her hoodie was lined with magnets and she knew that she had enough of them on her, that if McGregor attacked, he couldn't do the same damage to her as he'd done to Lenny.

She shuddered. The sun was fighting for supremacy over the fog, but so far, the heavy gray mist was winning – hands down. Mel couldn't believe that her phone forecast predicted Lunenburg would reach scorching temperatures that day.

She stopped and said a prayer before she opened the door. That done, she walked in and stood by the double-pillared entry and listened. Some of the cool fog from outside seemed to have attached itself to her and she shivered.

Even so, Josh and Dan had done their magic and everything appeared to be back to normal. She took a deep breath and walked to the middle of the foyer, closed her eyes and let her mind go blank, soaking in all the vibes and noises that only she could hear. If Edward knew about all her gifts, he might not be so receptive to her talents. She smiled, remembering the night before.

The staircase, with the stunning angel window, lay twenty-five feet in front of her. Feeling a chill, she moved into the dining room and closed her eyes... Again, nothing. She crossed the foyer and entered the large parlor.

Mel shivered again as cold spikes rippled up and down her spine. Hair stood up straight on her body and she felt the hairs on the back of her neck lift.

Mel stood in the middle of the room and pushed everything out of her mind.

"*Hello?* Is someone here?" she asked.

She moved around the room until she stood next to the twelve-foot-wide, white Italian marble fireplace that rose elegantly to touch the fourteen-foot ornate ceilings. She stepped forward to the rounded hearth and traced the carved verse with her finger. She read out loud: 'At journey's end, we will join hearts and hands forever'."

She was overwhelmed by a deep sadness for the man who had so much tragedy in his life, who'd lost so many people he loved and then turned this exquisite home into a mausoleum.

No wonder Emma's family loved the house overlooking the back harbor. Though it had been a home filled with memories and love, this beautiful house had also had more than its share of tragedies. And had little chance to be filled with laughter – rather had felt heartbreak and sorrow.

Mel sighed. "Oh, Archie Ramey... I feel so sorry for you and your loss."

Her heart caught in her throat. Someone was here in the

room with her. She sensed a presence. She sat down on one of the burgundy wing chairs by the fireplace and cleared her mind.

"Hello. Is anyone here?"

Nothing. Not a sound. She closed her eyes and emptied her mind and called out silently.

"Hello, is anyone here?"

A low whispering came through, but Mel couldn't make out any words. Just thoughts, and she knew that a spirit was present. And it wasn't McGregor because the specter was too weak to do any more damage now.

"Please, can you try harder to speak with me?"

In response, Mel heard soft sobbing. She felt that it was one of Archie's daughters, trying to contact her, but quickly her tingling subsided and the room took on its normal feel. Mel sensed this other spirit had something important to tell her.

What can it be? She carried a small occasional chair to the foot of the staircase in the foyer. Mel sat there with her hands on her lap and opened her mind again.

"Katie? Katie girl, are you there?" Mel focused with every-thing she had. *"Katie, can you speak with me? Where are you, Katie?"*

Mel thought that Katie wasn't going to answer, but as she stood up to take the chair back to the front room, a white mist began to take shape on the third wide step in front of her.

The white mist swirled and settled, forming a translucent Katie.

"Here I am, Miss." Mel could see the form of the little Irish lass in front of her and she
sighed with relief.

"Hello Katie. Are you okay?"

She felt the little ghost nod.

"Katie, what happened here yesterday?"

She could tell that the word, yesterday, was confusing for the little specter.

Mel thought quickly and changed the wording. *"Katie, what happened to make McGregor go berserk?"*

Clutching both hands to her chest, Katie began to rock in distress. *"I don't know, Miss, but it was somethin' fierce, it was. We all stayed hid. For fear of our lives."*

Mel had to smile, despite the situation. Katie believed she was still living in the real world, not realizing that she had died. Mel knew that a time would come soon that she could help Katie – and anyone else who lingered here – to cross over and finally find peace. But in this moment, she desperately needed to understand why McGregor was still on the prowl and getting stronger with each attack. The biggest and most important questions were, who called him and why?

"What happened, Katie?"

The mist on the stairs started to disappear.

"Katie honey, don't go. Come back. Katie can you hear me? I really need your help."

The mist swirled around the stairs and Katie's form emerged again.

Katie's voice was weak and terrified. *"Oh, Miss, he come from nowhere. Liftin' da furniture and crashin' it. We tried to keeps away from him, hidden upstairs, but he come from everywhere and..."*

Katie started to cry. *"Me and the mistresses huddled together, fearin' for our lives."*

Mel felt bad that she was reminding or scaring this poor, sweet spirit.

"Katie, don't cry. Please, don't cry. I promise, he can't hurt you. I can take you to a place where he'll never scare you again."

Katie wiped more transparent tears from her eyes with her long apron, shaking her head adamantly.

"No, Miss, I'm a stayin' right here with my missus. They need me. I'ms all dey got."

Mel smiled. So, it was the daughters of Archie Ramey that she had felt in the sitting room.

"Katie, did you notice anything before McGregor started his rampage?"

Katie nodded her head. *"Oh yes, Miss, the same tin happened every time we hear the door open and then out of nowhere that devil is upon us. He's sayin' words that me da would take him out behind the croft fer sayin'. They be so vile."*

Tears ran down her transparent face. *"I'm so afeared, Miss, I dun no know what to do."*

She began crying again and Mel could see the little form fading. Mel tried do reach out to her before she was gone, but the little specter was fading fast.

"Katie, do you know who enters the house before McGregor becomes so angry?"

Katie was fading fast. Mel thought she saw and felt Katie nod her head.

"I do, Miss. It's the same one every time. It was the..."

Mel strained, with all her being to hear what Katie was whispering, but she faded, leaving Mel frustrated and helpless. She had been so close to finding out who it was. But for now, she knew little more than she did before she spoke to the terrified ghost. Time was running out.

Her head turned quickly at the sound of the door opening. Edward stood in the fan-shaped entrance with his hands on his hips, glaring at her.

"What the hell are you doing here all by yourself?"

"And good morning to you. Boy, are you ever a grump in the morning."

Then Edward grinned at her. She knew he was thinking of last night.

That didn't last and he came back to the present glaring at Mel again, although she could tell his heart wasn't really in it.

"If you must know, I was having a little visit with Katie and it's called doing my job."

"Well you can forget about that because you're not doing this anymore."

She stood up abruptly and marched over to where he stood with his hands still on his hips. She faced him, crossing her arms, glaring at him. "Are you firing me, Mr. White?"

"Yes. I mean, no." He ran his hand through his hair. "I don't know what the hell I mean, Mel. When I saw you in here, I just couldn't believe it."

She smiled, in spite of herself, threw her arms around his neck and kissed him.

"Well, that makes me feel a little bit better, but I'm still angry with you, Mel. You almost gave me a heart attack when I saw you there."

"You're the second person today to tell me they almost had a heart attack."

Edward quirked his eyebrows. Her heart did a major flip flop. *What a handsome man.*

"Second? Who was the first, Katie?" When she didn't answer he asked again. "Katie? You were talking to a ghost, again?"

Mel nodded. "I did. I was trying to find out who is calling McGregor back from the depths of evil."

"What did you find out?"

"Well, Katie said every time they hear the door to the kitchen open they run and hide because they know that soon after that McGregor is going to go on the rampage again."

"The kitchen door?"

Mel nodded. "Apparently, whoever it is, enters the cellar from the kitchen and then summons our favorite monster."

Edward ran his fingers through his hair again. "I guess she didn't say who it was?"

Mel shook her head. "No, but she's still very afraid that McGregor's going to hurt her and her missus."

"*Missus?* What did she mean by that?"

"She means that you have at least four ghosts haunting this house."

Edward rolled his eyes. "Cripes. Isn't that just great."

Mel smiled at his discomfort. "It is, really. The three are no problem but the fourth one is McGregor and that's the one we have to get rid of, and quickly."

"And that's where I step in. I can't have you injured on my account. I'm going to contact my backers and inform them that this project is on hold, indefinitely."

Mel stood next to him, with her hands on her hips, staring at his determined face. "No, you're not."

He sighed. "Mel, I can't have this happen again. We almost lost Lenny. I sure as hell don't want anything to happen to the rest of my crew, especially you."

"Oh Edward, don't worry. I can look after myself."

They stood there for a moment facing each other. He pulled her into his arms and kissed her fiercely before drawing away. "I'm sorry. I never said good morning."

He kissed her again and she smiled.

"Good morning to you too, grumpy."

He beamed at her. "Maybe, it's because I didn't get very much sleep last night."

Dan came through the dining room as they separated. "Good morning. I checked the kitchen door and the lock was heavily scratched. Whoever did this is coming in through the kitchen."

Edward punched his fist into his palm. "Who the hell is it?"

Dan placed his computer briefcase down on the marble floor and looked around hesitantly.

Mel had to laugh at the frightened look on his face.

"It's okay, Dan. I just spent some time in here. McGregor is nowhere around."

Dan still checked out the large open foyer without moving too far inside. "How do you know?"

"Because I've been here for almost an hour and he's nowhere around. He did so much damage the last time that it's going to take a while to regenerate enough to appear again."

"Really, are you sure? How much time do we have?" Dan looked visibly relieved.

Mel looked very serious. "I'd say at least half an hour."

Both men looked at her, shocked.

Dan swallowed. "Cripes. Really?"

She laughed. "No guys, I'm sorry. Just some dark ghost-buster humor. I'd say it'll be at least a couple of days before he can cause any more havoc."

Dan scratched his head. "How are you so sure?"

Mel shook her head and played stupid. "I've seen it before. He's very dangerous, so as soon as you hear anything, like a bang or a crash or feel intense cold, drop everything and run for the door as fast as you can."

Josh came in from the dining room. "Don't worry, I'll be the first one out the door. I was never as scared as when I saw what happened to poor Lenny."

Mel nodded. "I mean it. If you notice anything, get out of here as fast as you can. This thing is dangerous."

Edward moved to the kitchen with Dan. Josh's phone rang.

He answered it.

Mel walked to the stairs, picked up the chair and carried

it back to the parlor. Re-entering the foyer, she watched Josh nodding his head. "Okay, I'll tell him."

Josh shouted to Edward in the kitchen. "Hey, Edward. L.A. just called. They tried to get you, but your phone kept going to message."

Edward poked his head around the pillars of the dining room.

"Damn, that's because I left it in the car. What did they want?"

"They said that Mrs. White was trying to call you and she couldn't reach you."

Edward nodded. "Okay, I'd better call her right away."

Edward smiled as he passed Josh in the foyer.

Mel quizzed Josh. "Mrs. White? His mother?"

Josh looked sheepish. "No..." He paused and looked at everything except Mel. "His wife."

Mel stopped and stared at Josh. She whispered, "His wife?"

Josh nodded. "She doesn't travel with him anymore, since she had her accident."

Mel licked her dry lips. "Accident?"

Josh nodded. "Yeah, it was really sad. She went for a run and a drunk driver hit her, hurling her into a ditch. She wasn't found until the next morning and by that time it was too late. She was paralyzed from the waist down."

"Oh my God, how awful."

"Yeah, it really was. She's a wonderful lady. Everyone loves her. I think it's been almost five years now since the accident."

Dan came through the kitchen door and entered the dining room.

Josh turned to him.

"Hey Dan, how long has Mrs. White been in the wheelchair?"

Dan thought for a moment. "As long as I've worked for the company. I'd say at least five years."

He picked up a roll of cable and left again.

Josh nodded, watching her face, then looked away. His look said everything. "I'd say it's been that long."

Mel wanted to get out of the house and away from Edward as soon as she could.

Josh grabbed another roll of cable from the floor. "So, Edward never told you about the accident?"

Mel snorted. "No, I think I would have remembered that. In fact, he never mentioned Mrs. White at all."

Embarrassed, Josh turned away. "Oh, I didn't know."

She opened the door and turned. "Umm, I have to go back to my room and make a conference call. Tell Edward I'll talk to him later."

She rushed from the house, almost running down the front steps, mumbling as tears blinded her eyes. "The lousy, cheating bastard."

Edward leaned against his car, speaking on his cell. He smiled when he saw Mel walking toward him and raised his hand for her to stop.

Blindly, she shook her head as she marched past, mumbling. "I'm in a hurry, Edward."

Almost running the last block toward the inn, she ignored Willow when she ran toward her. Mel ran up the stairs until she could hide behind closed doors.

"Stupid, stupid, stupid. When am I ever going to learn?"

After running up three flights of stairs and past the reception desk, she stopped, breathless, in front of her door.

Her hand shook so much, she could barely unlock the door.

Once inside, she sat down in front of her laptop and lost herself in a bout of weeping.

How could he lead me on so badly after he knew what I just went through?

After the weeping, Mel sat staring at a dark screen before going to the bathroom and placing a cold facecloth on her puffy red eyes. She smoothed moisturizer under her eyes, hoping to lessen some of the redness and swelling.

She stared at the mirror. "Right, that's helping a lot."

Her phone rang. Mel almost didn't answer because she knew who it was. She sighed deeply and a sob escaped from her throat, catching her breath. Taking another deep breath, she picked up the phone by the side of the bed.

"Hello, Mel Gordon speaking."

Aunt Jo's voice came from thousands of miles away.

"Mel honey, what's wrong? I know something is wrong. So, you may as well tell me."

Mel put her aunt on Skype. "Oh, Aunt Jo, I've been such a fool."

"What on earth happened, honey?"

"I just found out that Edward's married."

"Married, are you sure?"

Mel laughed mirthlessly. "Oh yes. And get this. She's been in a wheelchair for the last five years."

A long sigh escaped from her aunt. "I'm so sorry, Mel. Edward sounded amazing."

"Too amazing." Another dry sob escaped Mel's throat.

"Mel, you need to leave. I'll come down and finish the job for you."

Mel thought for a moment, then shook her head.

"Not on your life. I'm seeing this to the end."

Jo sighed. "I know it doesn't pay to argue with you. I know from experience, it isn't going to work. But, for what it's worth, I think he's a louse, dear."

Mel snorted. "Really? I hadn't noticed." She hated that she had feelings for Edward. "Oh, Aunt Jo, I really liked him a lot. In fact..." She paused and looked at the screen. "I'm in love with the married Edward White. He was everything that David wasn't, or so I thought. Boy, was I wrong. There must be a sign hanging over my head that says: easy target in flashing lights."

"Oh, honey, I'm so sorry. How are you going to handle this?"

"I'm going to be professional. That's how I was trained and that's what Mr. Edward White is going to get. Not one thing more."

"Really, honey? How will you handle being around him all day long? Come home and try to forget."

"Oh, Aunt Jo, I thought he was the one."

There was a pause on the other end. "I know honey. I could tell."

Mel had to smile, in spite of herself.

"I just bet you could."

She heard tapping on her door. "I have to go, Aunt Jo. I think the devil has come a knocking."

"Bye honey. Love you, and remember come home if you want to."

"No, that's not going to happen."

Mel took a deep breath and opened her door. Edward took one look at her swollen eyes and asked, "Mel, what happened?"

She smiled her brightest smile. "What? Oh, you mean my eyes. It's my allergies. There must be something around that's causing this. It happened earlier this year too."

"What can I do to help?"

"I have meds that I can take, so it will get better."

"Would you like to go for breakfast?"

Mel hesitated. "Oh, I don't think so."

He touched her eyes. "Put on sunglasses and no one will know the difference."

Mel sighed. "Okay, I'll be right down."

She took her glasses and put them on her head. "I think I'll be wearing these a lot."

She walked down to the lobby and smiled at the ghost couple.

Edward rose from his chair as she entered and pulled a chair out for her.

"I've ordered for both of us. The usual?"

"Yes, that's fine."

The waitress arrived with Mel's tea and Edward drank some of his coffee.

"I received a call this morning and I have to go back to L.A. for a couple of days. Will you be okay while I'm gone?"

"Oh, I'll be fine."

"Good. There's something I want to talk to you about when I get back."

Mel smiled sweetly and ate her toast. "I can hardly wait."

"What are you going to do while I'm gone?"

"I need to talk to Emma about the journal. There's something I'm missing."

"That sounds great and when I return, I'd like to take you for dinner someplace I know you're going to enjoy. I'd like to spend more time with you when I come back. Do you feel the same way, Mel?"

Her lips smiled but tears pooled behind the sunglasses. Oh, Edward, words cannot express what I'm feeling right now."

"Good. I'm glad to hear that."

He took her hand and held it. She pulled it from his.

"Now, I have news. I'm afraid that I must finish up in Lunenburg as soon as I can. I need to get back to the agency. So, I'll be working day and night to fix your problem. I'll see what I can find in the research reports I've been given. I need to find out who's been calling your ghost."

She glanced at her watch. "Which reminds me, I have some errands to do this afternoon." She pushed herself up from the table.

Edward rose and bent to kiss her cheek, but she moved away, leaving him kissing the air where she'd stood.

"Okay Mel, I'll see you when I return. I'll be back in two days. I should arrive in Lunenburg around six-thirty. Why don't we have dinner and you can give me a rundown of what you've found?"

Mel shrugged. "I'll see. Check with me when you return. Goodbye, Edward."

"Bye, Mel. Are you going back to your room? I'll walk you up."

"No, I need to go to the hardware store. They ordered more magnets for me."

"Oh, I'll take you there before I leave."

She shook her head, not looking at him. "Thanks, but I need to walk and think some things over. Have a safe trip, Edward."

He stood by the table watching her leave. His face full of confusion and hurt.

She reached the corner of the street where the Mourning Rose was located. Willow, the golden retriever, came bounding out of her doghouse when she saw Mel by the wrought iron fence.

Tears ran down Mel's face and she stooped to pet the dog through the spaces of the decorative, iron fence.

"Oh, Willow, don't ever fall in love. Men suck."

Willow barked and Mel hiccupped – a dry sob. "I'm glad you agree with me," she said, patting her head.

Edward's car passed her as he left town. He tooted the horn and waved. Mel kept petting Willow, ignoring his goodbye.

She walked back to the inn and waved at the ghostly

couple as she ran up to her room. Throwing herself on the bed, she sobbed herself to sleep.

———

Mel woke to the sound of the fog horn warning ships to beware.

She moved to the window and watched the heavy mist that hung over the town.

That morning she would call Emma. There must be something she was missing in the journal.

———

Emma passed Mel a beautiful china cup filled with fragrant Earl Grey tea, steaming to the brim.

"Enjoy your tea, Mel."

They sat out on the patio, overlooking the back harbor of Lunenburg. Mel looked around and sighed. "I love this house, Emma. It's so peaceful. It feels like arms wrapping around me."

Emma nodded as she placed a basket of blueberry muffins next to the steaming teapot in the center of the glass patio table.

"I know what you mean. I've always loved this house. I had that feeling when we'd come visit Gran. Even after she died, the house still felt the same. I'd come in and sit in the parlor in her old Boston rocker and wrap one of her quilts around me. It was almost like a big hug from her. Does that sound silly to you, Mel?"

Mel smiled and shook her head. "No, not at all. You were lucky that you had someone and something that helped to ease your loss."

Emma nodded her head. "I never felt lonely here. And

when the family decided to sell this place, I bought it. Number one reason, is because I wanted to keep it in the family and number two, sometimes I think that Gran is still here."

Mel shook her head. "She's passed over, Emma, but what she stood for and who she was has left lasting vibes that will never leave. She was so happy here with your grandfather and her children. This house is overflowing with love."

She smiled at Emma. "Something like that is hard to come by, and when it happens it never leaves that home."

Emma nodded. "That's why we sold the Ramey house. It never felt happy and you never wanted to sit and linger. I always felt so sad in that beautiful house."

Mel nodded. "I think it was because it never had a chance to produce good vibes. So much tragedy there in such a short time that for your family it could never be a happy place. Someone else needs to go and put their own imprint on that house and make it a warm and loving home."

Emma picked up the teapot and tipped it toward Mel. She nodded as Emma poured more golden nectar into Mel's cup, then filled her own.

Emma sighed as she placed the teapot back on the table. "I love these cups."

Mel nodded. "They're lovely."

"These cups are what great Uncle Archie would bring home to Annie, on his trips. She loved tea cups and he would find the most exotic ones he could for her."

Mel's purple peacock cup was balanced on a tripod. Peacock legs encircled the cup and the handle was a peacock's tail in full display.

Mel sipped from the translucent china. "I love this cup."

Emma smiled. "I'll wash it before you leave and you can take it home with you."

Mel shook her head. "Oh my gosh, I couldn't do that. It's so valuable."

Emma laughed at the look on Mel's face. "Mel, nobody drinks tea in the family, but me and I inherited Annie's entire teacup collection. All five hundred of them."

"*Five hundred?* Oh, my goodness. Five hundred?"

"A lot of them are still in boxes. I dug out the prettiest ones and I use them every day. I don't think I'm going to miss one teacup, since I have around twenty of the peacocks."

Mel smiled at her generous host. "In that case, I'll take it and use it all the time."

Emma saluted her with her teacup. "Every time you drink tea out of it, you'll remember Lunenburg. So, you won't forget us."

Mel kept the smile on her face, but her heart felt as fragile as the hundred-year-old cup she was holding. "Oh, I think I'll remember Lunenburg for a long, long time."

"I'll just go and wash it and then we can leave."

When Emma returned she passed Mel a small bag. "I've given you two peacocks."

"Oh Emma, I don't think I can take two."

Emma tilted her head to one side and laughed. "*Hmmm*, let me think. Two from five hundred leaves four hundred and ninety-eight. I think I can spare the other one. Then you can share your tea with someone special."

"Well, if you insist. How can I refuse? Thank you so much, Emma."

Mel opened her purse and took out her copy of the journal and placed it on the table.

"Emma, we have a huge problem at the house. Someone calls the spirit of McGregor back to this plane each time he comes. He's searching for something and he doesn't care who or what he hurts in his quest."

Emma – pouring more tea – froze with the pot in mid-air, shocked.

"What's he looking for and who could have called him?"

"That we don't know, but I was able to contact Katie and she says when he's on a rampage he keeps searching and shouting 'Where is it? Where is it?' I tried to ask Katie who is around at the time, but she faded away before she could tell me. I guess what I really want to know is who is calling McGregor back and if there is a treasure or something of value hidden in the house?"

Emma sighed. "I don't know. But, in the journal, Great-gran says that after the robbery of the bank, Archie wasn't happy putting all his money there. He had some quirky ways and that became one of them. I know when we sold the house to the production company, I felt guilty because Great-gran said in her journal, that the house was never to leave the family."

"I know. I read that, but did you ever hear why?"

"No, I always thought that it was a sentimental thing because of Archie. Maybe it was because of the window."

"The window?"

"The large one on the stairs."

Mel nodded. "What about it?"

"Well, after the girls were murdered, Archie had some company from Boston come down and build that window for him. It matches the stone that he had designed in the cemetery. You know that they're buried together in one casket? He had it specially made for them."

Mel sat in thought as Emma spoke. "I didn't know that there was a monument that matched the window."

"Oh yes, it's beautiful. When I was a little girl, I'd love to go and sit on the bench by the grave and look into the angel's face."

"Why?"

"I guess for the novelty of it; I never heard that angels could cry."

"How do you know that the angel is crying?"

"Because there's a plaque underneath the angel's foot that reads: Weep angel, weep for me. All the wealth in the world cannot mend a heart torn asunder."

Mel sighed. "He loved his daughters very much, didn't he?"

"The twins were a gift from his dying wife. They weren't expected to live, but they did. To lose them and his unborn grandchildren, I think is what killed him just months after they died."

Mel nodded. "Annie said, in her journal, that he became only a shadow of the man he used to be."

Emma nodded. "And that's how he died. A broken-hearted man who felt he had nothing to live for. It's very sad, isn't it?"

Mel nodded. "Yes, it really is."

They sat in companionable silence, letting the comfortable atmosphere of the house wrap its warmth around them.

Emma picked up the teapot and shook it. "Mel, would you like to have some more hot tea?"

Putting her hand up, Mel giggled. "If I have any more, I'm going to float away. I drank a lot of tea, even for me. And that's saying something."

Emma laughed. "I hear you. It's the cups. I'll make a pot of tea and then realize that it's empty. It's definitely the cup's fault." She carried the empty pot to the kitchen and poked her head around the doorframe. "Mel, would you like to see the stone?"

"I really would."

"It's on the back side of the cemetery, behind the Academy. We'll drive there together and then afterwards, I'll walk back. I like to walk in the morning and it's a good walk with all the hills."

Mel grinned. "After all the muffins I ate, I think I need the exercise."

————

When Mel braked the Jeep at the top of the hill, the old Lunenburg Academy stood before them. The Academy was the queen of all the dowagers of Lunenburg. Glistening in the mid-morning sun, it stood where most of Lunenburg could view its majestic visage.

Mel turned into the Academy yard. "Oh my gosh, how beautiful."

Emma agreed. "It is, isn't it? It was built as a school in 1896, at the height of Victorian architecture." She pointed to a road in the cemetery that circled the old school.

"Do you know what this area was called before the school was built?"

"No. What?"

"Gallows Hill."

"Gallows Hill?"

Emma nodded. "This is where they used to have the public hangings."

Mel stopped the car and they got out. She sensed this cemetery in Lunenburg was alive and well.

Two young girls walked hand in hand in the next lane by Mel's Jeep. She smiled sadly as they faded behind two small, mossy headstones.

She followed Emma down the slope of the hill and there, overlooking the back harbor, was an exact likeness of the angel window at the house. Only this angel, was carved in pure, white marble.

The floor, in front of the monument, was a marble slab

about fourteen feet square. Three cement benches lined the three sides of the little park. Pink rose bushes cascaded over white marble urns placed on either side of the angel.

Mel and Emma sat on one of the benches directly across from the statue.

The realism of the sculpture, took Mel's breath away. It was so lifelike one could expect the celestial stone angel to walk off her pedestal and join them on the bench.

"Oh my gosh, Emma. I thought that the stained glass angel was beautiful, but to see her standing here in front of us, carved in marble... it's overwhelming."

Emma laughed. "It is, isn't it? I've been coming here since before I can remember. And when things bother me, this is where I sit and try to work them out. It doesn't matter when I come, I always walk away feeling better. I think she's even more beautiful in the fall."

Two transparent little boys flitted under the sun-dappled trees.

Mel stared at Emma as she smiled at them. "Emma, can you see those two little boys?"

"I've been seeing them ever since I've been coming here. When I was small, I tried to play with them. One day, Gran saw me crying and asked what was wrong. I pointed to the little boys and said that they didn't want to play with me. Gran had to sit me down and tell me that I was seeing something that was no longer there. She took me over to where we saw them and knelt to read the stones. The stones identified them as two brothers. Albert and Ben. They both died from diphtheria on the same day."

"Oh, how sad."

"It was hard on families back then. Gran told me never to say anything to anybody about seeing them and it would just be our secret because Granny Em was the one, when she was little, that could talk to Katie."

Mel nodded. "I know how you felt, Emma. I was the same way, only I could speak with them. It must have been difficult to keep something like that from your friends. Thank God, I had my cousin, Kelsey, to confide in. We grew up together knowing that we could see and do things few other people could."

Emma nodded. "I never thought much of it. I just never told anyone what I could see. Gran was so good with me."

"She sounds like a special lady."

"She was the loveliest lady. She said that I was one of the people in the family that took after her and Great-gran Annie."

"Your great-grandmother could see ghosts?"

"Not only see them, but she knew when something bad was going to happen. Think that's the Irish in us. But I'm the only one in my family that has *this*, whatever it is."

Mel smiled. "In my family, most days we call it a gift, but a lot of times it seems more of a curse."

Emma sighed. "I know. It's not like you wake up one morning and say, gosh would I ever like to see ghosts today. Now, I can't talk to them. I can only see them. Gran knew something horrible was going to happen on the day that Archie left for England and she begged him to stay and leave another week."

"Yes. I read in her journal that she begged her brother not to go that day."

Emma smiled sadly. "As much as he loved his sister, he always pooh-poohed her beliefs and what she could do. That was another reason that he blamed himself so much for his girls' deaths. He remembered she begged him not to go – and he didn't listen to her because he didn't believe she had a real gift."

Emma stood up, wiped her jeans off and stretched. "I'd

better be going now. Bruce will be coming home soon and then we're off to New England for a few days."

Mel smiled up at her. "That sounds like fun."

"It is. We love to hit the antique shops."

"Do you look for anything special?"

"Not really. Bruce likes to look for old tools and I search for china teacups."

Mel snapped her head up and laughed. "You're, kidding. Right?"

Emma laughed at the expression on Mel's face. "Yes I am. I have enough cups to last me a lifetime, but I still love looking for them. It was so nice having tea with you this morning."

"Likewise. Have a good trip, Emma."

"Thanks, I'll talk to you when I return."

Mel, still facing the weeping angel, waved as Emma left. Her phone rang. She checked the caller. It was Edward.

She answered. "Hello, Edward."

"Great news, Mel. I just received word from the hospital that they're moving Lenny from ICU. He's going to be okay."

"Oh my gosh, Edward. That's wonderful. I'm so relieved."

"So am I, Mel. I called the guys. We have a lot to celebrate."

"I'm on my way home. I'll be back a day early. The business in L.A. wrapped up sooner than I thought. When I reach Halifax, I'll stop in to see Lenny. Then we need to talk, Mel. There's something you need to know."

She snorted to herself. *Oh brother. You got that one right.*

She had enough of the telephone call and of Edward.

"Mel, are you there?"

"I am, but you're breaking up, Edward. I'll see you when you return."

"Okay Mel. See you tomorrow evening. I can hardly wait

to see you again." There was a pause. "I'm hoping you feel the same way."

She didn't answer him.

She sighed deeply. Dear God, she wished with all her broken heart that she didn't feel the same way he did.

"Mel? Are you there?"

She couldn't speak to him, not now. "Edward, I can hardly hear you. We'll talk when you return."

"Okay Mel. Goodbye for now."

She broke off the connection before he could ask her again.

Sitting on the bench, she closed her eyes and tilted her face to feel the warmth from the midmorning sun. Two tears trickled unheeded down her cheeks. Two more escaped before Mel wiped away their wet path with the palm of her hand. She rose reluctantly and walked to her car.

Once inside, she glared at the steering wheel.

"So, Mr. White, you have something to tell me." She leaned back against the seat as a soft sob escaped her lips "Ya think?"

———

Mel walked to the front of the Ramey mansion and dragged herself up the first outside step. Why hadn't she left the hoodie off? Because she had sewn magnets onto every possible surface of the garment, even the hood. She was taking no chances. She grabbed the railing below the front door and pulled herself up to the stained glass entrance.

Leaning against the door, she breathed deeply. Man, she was either out of shape or these things were extra heavy. She looked around, catching her breath.

Yes. It was another lovely day in Lunenburg. The birds

sang from the branches of oak and maple trees that shaded the grounds around the house.

Rays from the early morning sun struck the windows of St. John's Anglican Church, morphing them into dancing hues of red and blue.

She pulled her sweater away from the front of her body. "Man," she mumbled to the door, "some of these magnets are sharp."

She had walked from the B&B, and because it was a cool morning, she'd worn the heavy hoodie instead of carrying it.

She mumbled to herself as she leaned on the door. "Oh Mel, you idiot. Why didn't you bring the Jeep?"

She unlocked the door and entered the cool foyer of the elegant home. She closed her eyes and listened. All was quiet.

Mel smiled. Not even her Katie was making a sound. She stood at the bottom of the steps and stared at the angel, identical to the marble seraph that stood guarding the twins' graves in the cemetery.

Walking through the double marble arches of the dining room, she stopped and listened again.

Silence.

She moved through to the kitchen, where she stopped and closed her eyes again. Not a twinge or a stir. Through the window, she watched the sun cut through the fog and rise above the lighthouse on the Battery.

The fog horn blared, warning sailors and fishermen that all was not well. The mournful sound tugged at her heart.

She sighed. "I'm going to miss this."

Standing by the grand staircase, she closed her mind to everything and tried to summon Katie.

"Katie, are you there? Katie can you hear me?"

Softly, so softly she barely heard a whisper. *"Not now, Miss. Not now."*

"Katie, I want to talk to you."

Katie screamed in her mind. *"Run Miss. Run."*

Too late. Glacial air swirled around her.

Terrified, Mel turned from the stairs to run. She couldn't move. Whatever it was, held her there. Slimy, wet fingers slithered across her face. Bile rose in her throat, as foul putrid air surrounded her.

Mel kicked out at the air, as she was lifted and thrown, then slid into a corner. Taking great gulps of air to defuse the pain, she pulled herself up on her hands and knees.

Gagging from the smell that encompassed the room, she swallowed hard and willed herself not to throw up.

Dear God. What was happening? Why aren't the magnets working?

"Holy Mother of God. Run, run, run." Katie screamed each word into her head.

A wooden settee was hurled through the air toward her and upon impact, Mel collapsed again on the floor, and blackness engulfed her.

Katie's scream was the last thing she heard.

13

"Mel? Mel are you okay?"

She heard Josh's voice from far away. "Oh my God, Dan. Is she dead?" someone asked.

"No, but she's banged up pretty bad."

Mel whispered. "Please don't shout. My head is killing me."

Dan touched Mel's shoulder. "Mel, are you okay?"

"I-I don't know." She tried to touch the back of her head, but searing pain pulsed up her arm and she moaned with the effort.

A short distance from where Mel lay sprawled on the floor, broken pieces of wood that resembled a splintered settee were strewn about.

Dan looked around. "What the hell happened here?"

She tried to sit up and they moved to help her into a sitting position.

"I ran into McGregor." She moved around cautiously, holding her arm to lessen the pain. "Or a train."

Dan took her head in his hands and gently turned it from

side to side. He checked her pupils with a small light, grinning at Josh.

"I told you these little lights would come in handy. Now, let's take off your jacket, Mel, and see what your arm looks like. We'll help you up and sit you on something comfortable."

Josh ran and came back with a velvet parlor chair.

They eased her onto the seat.

Josh leaned over. "Are you okay, Mel?"

"I'm not sure. I think so."

Dan helped her off with her hoodie, staring at it, confused. "This jacket must be a new fashion statement."

"It's full of magnets. They keep the ghosts from attacking. They have a magnetic field that spirits don't like."

Dan smiled, as he eased her arm out of a sleeve. "I think you should go somewhere else for your supply. These really suck."

Mel laughed, despite the throbbing pain in her head and arm.

"No, Dan, you're wrong. They really worked. He tried to attack me, but he couldn't because of the force field that these magnets created. So, he did the next best thing. He came as close to me as he could and then picked up a chair and threw it at me for all he was worth. He couldn't stay close to me for long. The magnets drained his energy."

She winced when he touched her arm.

"Relax Mel, I'm a trained paramedic. I served overseas for two stints. I can promise you that I've had to look at worse than this."

He looked at her arm, moving it up and down, even when Mel gave a sharp moan.

"You are one lucky lady. Nothing's broken, but you're going to have some wild bruises on your arm."

He looked at her and smiled. "Are you okay with my diagnosis or would you rather go to the hospital and get them to check you out?"

"I think I've already had the best diagnoses I could get, so I'm fine with that."

"I want you to go back to your room and rest. Take a nap, or at least lie down. I'll check on you throughout the day."

She started to argue with him and he put his hand up, interrupting her.

"Mel, it's my way or the hospital. Now make your decision."

He helped her up. "Okay, let's do this slowly. You're banged up quite a bit."

Josh came through the door and helped Mel to her feet.

"Josh, I'm driving Mel back to the inn."

"I'm fine, Dan. I just need to rest for a bit and I need to check on something. Can I work on my laptop when I get to my room?"

"That's up to you. I'd have a lie down first and then see how you feel later this afternoon."

He helped her to the door.

Josh stood, watching them leave, his face full of concern.

"Hope you feel better soon, Mel."

"Thanks, Josh."

Dan drove her to the inn and helped her up the stairs to her room. Taking the key from her hand, he unlocked the door.

He whistled, looking around. "Nice place. Ours is nice too, but this is classy. Josh and I have rooms on the second floor."

She laughed. "I wondered where you were."

He looked around. "Now, lie down and rest. Do you have any pain meds?"

"In the bathroom."

"Well, take something and you should be right as rain."

And she did.

———

Mel lay for some time, restless and uncomfortable. After taking more meds, she decided to Skype Aunt Jo.

"Hi, honey."

"Hi Aunt Jo, I need you to come here as soon as possible."

"How many of us do you want?"

"I need you and Kelsey."

"Thank God, you've come to your senses. Something happened, didn't it?"

"Mel nodded at the screen. I had my loaded hoodie on and the thing was able to pick me up and throw me. Then it threw a chair at me from twenty feet. If it hadn't been for Katie screaming at me to leave, I would have been seriously hurt from the impact of that heavy piece of furniture."

"Mel, are you sure you're okay?"

"Well, I have a bad bruise on my arm and a lump on my head, but other than that, I'm okay."

"Did you go to emerg?"

"No, I have my own paramedic. He's a sweetie and he's looking in on me off and on all day."

Her aunt sighed at the other end. "Well, that makes me feel better. I'd better go and arrange things. I'll call and let you know when we're arriving."

"I don't want McGregor hurting any more people. He's going down, and hard."

"That's my girl. We'll be there as soon as we can. Bye honey. Love you."

"Love you too."

Feeling relieved that she would have a team working with her, Mel lay down and finally allowed the medication to do what it was supposed to do.

———

"Mel. Mel it's time to wake up."

She opened her eyes to see Dan smiling, standing by her bed.

She closed her eyes again.

"Mel?" Dan shook her gently. "Mel, you should wake up now. How long were you asleep?"

Mel pushed the quilt from her body and gingerly pulled herself up into a sitting position on the edge of the bed.

Glancing at the clock on the night table, she sighed. "Oh, I think about an hour."

"That's fine. How's the head?"

"Mel cautiously moved her neck back and forth. "I think it's fine. I took some meds before I lay down the last time. It helped a lot."

He touched her arm. She gasped.

"Well, that answers that question. Now, I want you to come downstairs and have something to eat."

"Okay, Doc, Thanks. I'll be down in a little bit."

"Good. We're waiting for you in the dining room. Don't be long. You need something in your stomach other than the meds you took."

———

A few minutes later, Mel walked into the dining room and stopped short. Standing, with a chair pulled out, was the group, including a beaming Edward.

Plastering a smile on her face, she walked toward the table of concerned men.

Edward moved to meet her, enveloping her in an embrace. Just for a moment, she lost herself in his arms. She knew, with all her heart, they felt the same way about each other, but that this was as far as it could go. They could never be together.

His face filled with concern, as she winced.

"Mel, are you okay? The guys just told me what happened. I wanted to come to your room, but Dan said that you were on your way down to have a meal with us."

"I'm fine, Edward. It's not the first time I've had something thrown at me, but I've never had anything that heavy thrown with such force."

He pulled her chair out and she nodded to the waitress as she hovered with a teapot. She sipped the hot nectar and sighed, smiling at her guys who hung on every word she said.

"All is right with the world. I have my tea." She took another sip and then poured more into her cup. "Gosh, I really needed this."

Mel caught the look of concern on all their faces. "Guys, I'm okay. You do not want to know what I've had thrown at me over the years. This is nothing, I promise you."

Edward took a deep breath. "I was sick with worry."

"Edward, I'm fine. Just one of the hazards of the job. I thought you weren't coming until this evening."

"I was able to get an earlier flight." He took her hand and she let him hold it just because she didn't want to make a scene in front of Josh and Dan, but mostly because his touch felt wonderful.

"Edward, please stop fussing. I'm okay. This is what I do for a living and sometimes things happen. This was one of those times. So, let's enjoy the meal. I'm starved."

Dan laughed. "She's going to be fine."

Toward the end of the meal, when everyone was filled with food and laughter, Edward's phone rang. He glanced at caller ID and then around the table. "It's the hospital."

"Hello, Edward White speaking." He paused and gazed at Mel. "Yes, Brenda."

Everyone held their breath, scanning Edward's face, waiting for what he'd say next.

"What? When?" He paused and beamed at them. "That's great, Brenda. Thank you. Thank you so much. Goodbye."

His grin said it all. "That was Brenda Conrad. Lenny's been moved from ICU into a private room."

Josh and Dan hooted and gave each other a fist pump.

Dan pumped his arm in the air. "Man, oh man, that's great news."

Josh leaned his head way back and laughed. "Way to go, Lenny."

Mel wiped tears from her eyes and laughed as Josh gave the confused waitress a hug. "Linda, we just heard the best news about Lenny. He's going to be okay."

Linda smiled at them. "Oh, I'm so glad. He's such a nice guy. I'll tell the other staff."

Josh stood up. "Edward, we're going to Halifax to see Lenny and when we return we're going to sit down and have a meeting. We should decide who will crew the series. What did L.A. tag this one?"

"The working title is the same as the movie, *Beyond the Mist*."

Dan nodded. "Sounds good. Okay, see you when we return."

What followed was a mass exodus of the guys and Mel realized that she was alone with Edward at the table, sitting too close together.

Mel sighed. "Well. I should go."

She moved to leave the table, but Edward touched her arm. "Mel, we need to talk, please."

She sighed and looked sadly at this man, who she knew loved her as much as she loved him. Finding out he had a wife and that he hadn't been honest with her about his marriage, was not acceptable.

"Edward, I said that we would talk when this assignment was over. I need reinforcements. I've asked Aunt Jo – along with whoever else she can bring – to come work with me. There're flying in soon and I've things to do before they arrive. Now, that you've decided there's going to be more filming at the house, we need to get rid of this monster, and fast. I have to put all my energy into this, and I promise, we'll talk right after."

"But Mel, there's something I want to say to—"

She put her hand up, shaking her head. "Edward, please. Not now. I have to go upstairs and get ready for the gang before they land here." She stood up. "I need to book rooms for everyone."

"I'll do that for you. How many rooms do you need?" Mel thought for a moment. "Probably two."

"That's not a problem, Mel. I've quite a few rooms booked so, I think that we already have enough for your crew."

Mel smiled down at him. *What a kind and thoughtful man. Why the hell does he have to be married?* "That's great. Thank you."

She pushed her chair away from the table and stood up. Edward jumped up and pulled her into his arms. "I never thought I'd ever say I'm glad my place is haunted. I never would have met you otherwise, Mel."

Tears ran down her face as he held her in his arms. She closed her eyes, trying hard to memorize this moment. The tears flowed down her cheeks unheeded. She pulled out of his embrace and tried wiping them away.

He smiled and wiped a tear before it trickled off her chin. Taking a hanky from his breast pocket, he wiped her eyes.

"Oh no. Your allergies?"

Mel nodded. "I guess so."

He touched her chin and smiled. "Gosh Mel, I hope

you're not allergic to me. Can you do anything about the tears?"

She smiled sadly. "I can. And the treatment I'm taking will stop them in a few days."

He touched her lips gently with his thumb, then pulled her closer.

Oh God, she wanted that kiss so bad, but she couldn't let it happen. Mel knew she needed to get away from him and fast, before she became a blubbering idiot in his wonderful arms. Before she blurted out things she didn't want to say to him right now. Certainly not in the middle of the dining room.

She pulled away from him. Stooping, she retrieved her purse from the table. "If you would look after the rooms for me that would be great."

He nodded. "And, as soon as this is behind us, we need to talk. I'm hoping you can fly out to L.A. and we can spend some time together."

She sighed deeply. "We'll see. I need to go now and get ready. Goodbye, Edward."

She strode to the reception area and down the front steps to the Jeep. She mumbled to herself. "Dear God, he wants to see me in L.A."

She snorted in disgust. "There's something about me you don't know, Edward White. Mel Gordon does not, and would never, encroach on another woman's husband, especially a wife that's been shackled to a wheel chair for five years."

14

M el's phone rang.

"We're here," Aunt Jo announced.

Mel ran down the last flight of stairs by reception and almost flew into her aunt's arms. "Aunt Jo. Oh my gosh, it's so good to see you."

Her aunt, an attractive woman in her late fifties, took Mel in her arms and hugged her hard. "How are you doing, honey?"

"I'm fine."

Her aunt's eyes studied her.

"No, really I'm okay. I just want to get this over with and do the best job I can for Edward."

She looked around. "Did anybody else come with you?"

"Kelsey's outside by the rental, getting our luggage sorted."

She ran outside and watched as her cousin Kelsey held a clipboard and stood checking the luggage with one of the inn's employees. "Okay, that goes to Aunt Jo's room."

Kelsey turned around and beamed as Mel ran toward her. "Oh, Mel, it's great to see you."

She looked deep into Mel's eyes, as she hugged her. "You okay?"

Mel nodded. "I'm so glad you guys are here." She smiled broadly. "I'm fine; don't worry about me. I'm a tough Gordon."

"Hello, it's me you're lying to, but you are a survivor."

Mel nodded. "You don't know the half of it."

The family resemblance was uncanny. The girls standing side by side could have been mistaken for twins except Kelsey had long curly blond hair and Mel's auburn hair fell in heavy waves to her shoulders.

Edward drove up behind the rental as the trunk was unloaded.

He walked over to the group and smiled. "I see the reinforcements have arrived."

"Edward, this is my Aunt Jo and my cousin Kelsey. This is Edward White, our boss."

He shook their hands. "Welcome to Lunenburg. I just wish we were meeting under more social circumstances. Now let's get your luggage stowed away and then I want to take you all out for dinner."

Mel chuckled to herself as she looked at the luggage piled on the sidewalk. He had no idea how hard it was going to be to get her aunt and her cousin settled. They did not travel light.

She grinned as Edward pulled out the last heavy suitcase from the back of their rental. "Wow. What's in here, rocks?"

Aunt Jo grinned. "No, my proton pack."

Edward stopped abruptly. And stared at her. "Really?"

She laughed. "No Edward, I'm joking."

He smiled at Mel. "I've been the butt of that joke before. You'd think I'd have learned by now."

Jo laughed at his expression. "FYI Edward, we don't have proton packs. We never had them, but we can't resist pulling people's legs with that one." She smiled and touched his arm. "Sorry, it's just too hard to resist."

By then, the last of the suitcases stood in front of the reception desk.

Angie smiled. "We have rooms for you, just down the hall."

Aunt Jo and Kelsey smiled at the ghostly couple that walked arm in arm across the reception area, toward the dining room.

Mel sighed in relief. "Wow, that's great. You're on the first floor." Settling her family should be relatively easy, but Aunt Jo had a way of complicating things. Most things.

Edward helped with the luggage, checked to make sure that they were happy with the room arrangements and then after he dumped the last suitcase in front of Jo's bed, he looked around and took a deep breath. "Now, let's go for dinner."

Dinner was not as uncomfortable as Mel thought it would be. Edward kept them laughing at his stories about dealing with the trials and tribulations of Hollywood's rich and famous.

Mel loved him even more because of the time he spent making her family feel comfortable.

Their food arrived and she laughed at the look on the faces of the lobster virgins when they took their first bite.

Kelsey chewed slowly on her butter-dipped lobster. "Oh my gosh, where have you been all my life?"

Aunt Jo laughed at the look on her face. "It's really delicious, isn't it?"

Edward tilted his head back and roared. "Kelsey, you have the same look on your face that Mel had when she had her first bite."

Kelsey's eyes rolled. I can feel the pounds packing on now."

Mel snorted. "You don't have to worry about the pounds if you walk anywhere in Lunenburg. The place is built on a mountain."

Aunt Jo nodded. "I noticed that. My morning run should prove interesting."

Edward announced: "Dessert has arrived."

Kelsey groaned. "I can't eat another bite."

Edward and Mel smiled at each other. He leaned over the table. "I bet you will."

He put his fork down after scrapping the last of the lemon sauce from his plate. "I want to thank you both for coming to help in this situation."

Jo smiled as she pushed her coffee cup aside.

"Edward, you hired the Gordon Agency to stop the destruction on your movie sets. Whether it's one, three or nine members of the agency on the job, we finish what we set out to accomplish."

Kelsey nodded. The last job was a doozy. "We had seven spirits that we had to get rid of."

"Seven?"

Jo sighed. "It took three of us, three weeks, day and night before we sent them on their way."

She checked her watch. "I'm ready for bed. Thank you, Edward, for this amazing meal. I want to have a run tomorrow morning before we tackle your problem."

Kelsey stretched. "It really has been a long day."

Edward took the highway back to Lunenburg and parked close to the front door of the inn.

He touched his pocket. "Excuse me just for a moment, I should take this." He held the phone to his ear. "Hello, yes?"

He paused and Mel could tell that the news wasn't good. "What? When did it happen? Yes?" He listened intently.

Sighing, he ran his hand through his hair. "Okay, I'll be there as soon as I can. Thanks, Mona."

He noticed the concern on their faces.

"Sorry ladies, I'm afraid I have to go to L.A. I wish I could be here with you, but it's an emergency."

Jo nodded as she followed Kelsey up the steps. "Don't worry Edward, we can handle this without you. Thank you for the lovely dinner and good night."

They entered the inn, leaving Edward and Mel alone.

He touched her cheek. "I'll be back as soon as I can."

Mel felt as though she had turned into a statue. She knew "emergency" was just another word for wife.

He watched the ladies enter the inn, before facing her. Taking her hand in his he whispered, "Mel, have I done or said something? Is it David? I know how badly he hurt you. What's wrong?"

Tears threatened to escape from the corners of her eyes. "Right now, I don't think I can handle dealing with the kind of relationship you want from me." She smiled sadly and slipped her hand from his. "We'll probably be gone before you return. This is likely goodbye, Edward."

She left him standing on the sidewalk alone and walked away. Afraid that if the words came tumbling from her lips, she would never be able to retrieve them and he would know how much she really loved that kind, funny, gentle man she'd recently learned belonged to another woman.

———

Mel tapped on Jo's door, placing a smile on her face, before she entered.

They looked up from where they were filling the pockets of their hoodies with magnets.

She beamed at them. "Are you guys getting settled?"

Jo nodded. "Yes dear, we're just placing our work clothes out for tomorrow."

Later, Mel stood by her open window with only the dim light from a Victorian street lamp lighting her room. She took a deep breath of the damp, salty fog that seeped through her lace curtains.

Again, a fog horn echoed mournfully from the harbor. A knock sounded on her door. Every muscle in her body tensed to its breaking point.

"Mel, are you in there? It's Edward. We really need to talk. Mel?" Her body stiffened. She stood by the darkened window holding her breath, waiting for another knock — one that never came.

Blinded by tears, she whispered, "Oh, please Edward, not now."

Instead she sobbed alone in her room. Minutes later she watched from the safety of her darkened room as Edward stared up at her bedroom window before driving away into the fog-filled night.

———

Jo stood with her nieces in the center of the foyer. "Edward owns a gorgeous house. How many ghosts?"

Mel smiled, nodding. "Well, there's Katie. She's here because she feels she has to protect her mistresses — Archie's two daughters, Emma and Olive. I can feel a whisper of them occasionally. I think they're stuck here, because of the trauma surrounding their deaths."

Jo nodded. "Without a doubt. Those poor souls have been here long enough. When this is over, we'll help them on their way too."

A screeching wail caught them off guard. "What in the hell was that?"

Mel grabbed them. "Oh my God, that's McGregor. How can he be back so soon?"

Jo took Mel's hand. "Where is he? Can you tell where the noise is coming from? I can't."

Mel shook her head. Over the screaming, she shouted to her aunt, "I don't know."

Kelsey leaned toward her so she could hear her. "What's it saying?"

Jo, with her hands over her ears, shook her head. Kelsey grabbed both women by the arms and shouted at the top of her voice. "I think it's saying, 'It's mine. It's mine.'"

Mel and Jo nodded in agreement.

They stood together in the center of the foyer. Kelsey pointed to the dining room. "Look, over by the window."

There in front of the stunning peacock window, a black mist swirled and wove back and forth.

With revulsion, they watched as the swirling, dark mist took shape. Became a form that had Mel almost rooted to the floor. It once was a man. She could almost see the shape of his face. The stench was gagging as the huge shadow began moving toward them. Staggering slowly from side to side. A demonic toddler, taking its first steps.

The noise it made was deafening. Piercing screams so loud, windows vibrated from the intensity of them.

Mel grabbed Kelsey's and Jo's arms, pulling them toward the door, as the first airborne chair flew toward them, missing Jo by inches.

Another frustrated blood-curdling scream rent the air, followed by another chair smashing into pieces on the wall beside them.

A broken wooden arm of one hit Kelsey on the leg. "Damn, that hurt."

Mel grabbed their arms more tightly. "Come on, let's get out of here. I've seen what he can do and I don't want to be around again for the main performance."

Jo stood her ground, staring at the monster "I want to see what he does next."

Mel grabbed her arm, shaking her head. "No, you don't. Now, Aunt Jo. Now."

The shadow from hell moved closer to where they stood watching it in horror.

Jo grabbed their hands and shouted above the screaming. "Amazing, I've never seen one with this much energy."

McGregor's essence bent over and picked up a fern stand with both hands, holding it eight feet above the floor, all the while screaming. "It's mine! It's all mine!"

"That's our cue to get out of here." Mel dragged them by their arms to the open door, shutting it behind them just before the stand crashed against the other side.

They ran to the sidewalk, shocked by what they had just witnessed.

Jo shook her head. "In all my years doing this, this is the first time I've been so frightened I wanted to run away."

A car pulled up. Josh and Dan jumped out and ran to join them.

Josh grabbed Mel's arm. "Why are you standing out here?"

Mel pointed with her head to the house. "Listen."

Dan's jaw dropped at the commotion inside. "Are you ladies okay?"

Mel nodded. "We're fine, Josh. One more minute inside and I'm not sure we'd be able to say that."

Numb, they stood listening to the screaming and wailing of the heinous specter that rampaged inside, just steps from where they stood. Another piece of furniture crashed against the door.

Dan, his face pale, stared at Mel. "Jeeze, how long can this go on?"

Jo checked her watch. "It can't last much longer. He's been at this for almost seven minutes."

No sooner had Jo uttered the words, when the screaming and pounding stopped. The sound of silence filtered through the open window to where five people stood huddled together on the sidewalk.

Kelsey cocked her head to the side. "I think it's done."

Mel raised her hands in the air. "What kind of energy does it have − for heaven's sake? Oh, where are my manners? Aunt Jo and Kelsey, meet Dan and Josh."

They shook hands. "So, you're the men that have been babysitting my niece?"

Kelsey grinned. "Good luck with that."

Jo moved toward the door. "I'm going to find out where it's getting its energy."

"Wait." Dan ran up and stood beside her at the door. "You can't go in there. It's not safe."

Josh, sprinted up behind Dan and joined them on the steps.

"Lady, are you nuts? Listen to Dan."

Jo smiled at them both. "Some people think I am. Nuts I mean. But really, it's safe now. He's used up most of his energy."

She tried to open the door, but it only budged a few inches. "I can't open it. Something's up against it."

She turned to the men. "I need some strong men to push the door open for me. Some of the furniture must be wedged against it."

Dan sighed deeply. "Okay, if you're sure this is wise." He sighed again and stood in front of Jo, in protection mode. "Stand back. I'm not very happy about this."

She laughed and touched Dan's shoulder. "Really, I hadn't noticed. I promise, he − or whatever it is − is gone. It won't be back for a while."

Mel and Kelsey followed close behind their aunt. Dan and Josh reluctantly followed the ladies at a distance.

Josh looked at Dan and mumbled. "I don't like this. I don't like this at all."

Inside, they found complete and utter destruction.

They pushed through the broken side tables and occasional chairs that lay on the floor and against walls.

Josh pointed to the corner of the parlor. "Man, oh man. Would you look at that? From now on Dan, we have to return the furniture to the warehouse after we do the sightings with the long-range cameras. We're going to run out of furniture soon if this keeps up."

The women walked around the bottom floor, moving back and forth between the dining room and foyer. Every piece of furniture that was moveable had been smashed against the wall or against larger furniture that was too big to damage. A seat and back of a chair hung precariously on the top of a large china cabinet.

Broken furniture legs dangled from chair frames, entwined with splintered table tops that lay, as if discarded.

It was as if a spoiled child, tired of its doll house furniture, had thrown it on the floor.

Josh sighed. "Come on Dan, let's clean this mess up. I'll get some boxes. Lately I feel more like a janitor than a producer."

The women walked together, trying to detect where this monster was coming from and where he'd gone.

Mel shook her head. "I've never seen such destruction from one apparition. Have you seen this before, Aunt Jo?"

Jo nodded. "Remember Mel, in Phoenix I had to call your mother to help me. We had three specters that were ripping an old museum apart. They did a major job, but here, it's only one. She looked at Kelsey. Why is it so strong? Can you pick anything up?"

Kelsey frowned. "Not a thing. It seems like a strong thick wall in front of me."

Jo stared at her. "You mean you're being blocked?"

Kelsey nodded. "Big time."

Mel looked around. "This isn't the first time he's caused so much destruction, but this is major. He seems to be gaining a lot of strength – and fast."

Josh, dragging boxes, came down the stairs and joined them. "You should see what he did upstairs the last time. Hey Dan, why don't you take the ladies to the second level and show them the fun it had on his last rampage." He shook his head at Aunt Jo. "It's a doozy."

Dan rolled his eyes and nodded at Jo. "Swear to me he's not coming back."

Jo laughed in spite of herself. "I cross my heart, Dan. He won't be back. Not for a while anyway."

Rolling his eyes again, he motioned with his hands. "Okay ladies, follow me."

He led them up the staircase to the second floor.

Josh moved to where Mel stood and began picking up large chunks of broken furniture.

She took a measuring tape from her pocket and began measuring the distance from where McGregor started and how far the furniture had landed. "Wow. What a lot of energy."

Josh held the tape for her. "Am I ever glad that Edward wasn't here to see this."

She nodded.

He checked the numbers on the tape measure. "Okay, this says fifteen feet."

Mel wrote it down. "That's amazing."

Josh snorted. "Yeah, well I'm glad you think so. Dan said that Edward called this morning. That everything went well in L.A."

Mel stopped and stared at Josh. "Oh, I didn't know why he had to leave. He told me an emergency came up. We were just finishing dinner when he took the call. He left for the airport shortly after that."

She didn't tell Josh that she watched Edward drive away, or that it had torn her heart apart. She'd keep that little secret to herself.

"They called Dan and told him Mrs. White fell from her wheelchair when it rolled down the patio steps."

"Oh no? Is she okay?"

Josh shrugged. "I don't know. I didn't hear."

Mel looked up from her clipboard as Jo and Kelsey, followed by Dan, descended the stairs.

Josh passed the tape measure back to Mel. "Dan? Did Edward tell you when he was returning to Lunenburg?"

"He said he was leaving tonight. Be back early tomorrow."

"Hey Dan, how's Mrs. White?"

"She's doing fine."

Josh grinned. "That's great. What an awesome lady. She never complains about anything, but she really misses Edward when he's on location."

Mel smiled for the benefit of the men and took out her measuring tape to measure an end wall outside the dining room. If she heard Mrs. White one more time, she was going to scream louder than McGregor.

She walked to the dining room and measured a wall that didn't need any attention.

Oh Edward, what are we going to do?

Jo and Kelsey nodded to Mel then turned to the men. "Okay guys, you need to go now."

The men stared at her. "What do you mean? We need to leave *now?*"

Mel waved both her hands.

"No, I mean we have to go to work and you have to leave."

"What?" Dan stared at her. "Woman, are you insane? We're not going to leave you here alone in this house."

Jo and Kelsey walked over and stood by the men.

Mel put her hands on her hips. "Yes, you are. It's our job and we can't have civilians around us when we're working. You might get hurt."

Josh shook his head. "Edward would have me fired and run out of town if I didn't look after you while you're here in this hellhole."

Kelsey moved in front of them and opened the door wide for the men to leave. It was a dismissal they didn't miss.

"We can't do our job if we have to worry about what's happening to you, so please leave. We'll be just fine."

Josh glared at Mel. "I don't like this."

She smiled at the concern etched on both men's faces. "Don't worry guys. Now goodbye. We'll see you soon. I promise."

She glanced at her watch. "We'll meet for lunch at the wharf. We've done this before. We'll be okay."

She opened the heavy door even further and swept her hand toward the opening. "Now scoot."

Josh and Dan shrugged their shoulders and reluctantly dragged themselves to the door.

Standing on the threshold, Dan turned. "Please, come with us."

Josh put his hands on his hips. "It's not safe for you in here."

Mel nodded as she gave them a gentle shove and began closing the door on them. "You're right. It isn't safe. That's why you need to go."

Dan put his hands out to keep the door open. "All I can think of is Lenny and I don't want the same thing happening to you."

Mel sighed. "Lenny isn't a trained professional in the paranormal. We are. Final time. Goodbye."

She closed the door in their faces.

Kelsey grinned, her back against the door. "Wow, talk about being overprotected."

15

After closing the door on the men, Mel sighed. "Okay. Let's get started."

Closing her eyes, Jo leaned against the polished wood of the staircase's banister. "Someone's here with us, but they're not coming forward."

Mel smiled. "That's Katie. She's the one I told you about that's staying back to protect her mistresses. I'd try to bring her forward, but she's very timid. I'm afraid with both of you here, she might not make an appearance."

Aunt Jo waved her hand. "That's fine, dear. She's probably terrified after that last episode anyway."

Kelsey walked around. "I'm detecting another presence, but it's so weak, I'm not picking up very much."

Jo closed and then opened her eyes. "Why don't we try to contact Katie a little later, after she's had time to calm down. I agree with Mel; we're not going to have any conversations with her now – that's a given."

Mel took a deep breath and opened the backpacks that they'd placed next to the dining room, earlier. "Okay, we need to find McGregor's portal and fast. This has gone on long enough." She looked at her cousin and aunt. "We must set a trap."

Mel led the way through to the kitchen and down the rickety steps to the large room at the foot of the stairs.

She turned around on the steps. "I'd say hang on, but there doesn't seem to be much to hang on to. These steps haven't been replaced since the house was built over a hundred years ago."

Jo's light danced around the dirt floor, flickering around the empty room. "I see what you mean. I'm betting this room was never featured in *Homes of Lunenburg*."

Kelsey sniffed the air. "Can you smell that? He's been here or close to this room."

Mel moved toward the door on the side opposite the steps. "It's this way."

They entered single file and moved along the long, damp, narrow corridor.

Jo sniffed. "The smell is a lot stronger here than out by the steps. This is how he's traveling."

Mel pulled the zipper of her hoodie, heavy with magnets, to the top of her neck. "Okay, let's make sure that he can't get near us."

Kelsey squeaked in alarm. Jo and Mel instantly turned their lights on her.

She smiled sheepishly at them. "Sorry guys, I ran into a cobweb. Did I tell you how much I hate spiders?"

Jo chuckled. "I think you've mentioned it a few times over the years, dear. Now Mel, where do we go? I'm guessing we follow our noses. It's becoming stronger."

"It's just over..." Mel's light flickered and died.

The smell of sulfur and molasses surrounded them.

Mel shook her flashlight. "This shouldn't have happened. I just replaced all the batteries yesterday."

Kelsey swore. "Damn, mine's gone out too."

The corridor took on an eerie glow, with only Jo's light dimly lighting McGregor's lair.

Jo passed Kelsey her light, pulling her backpack from her shoulder. "Shine it on my bag, honey. We don't have much time... Okay, it looks like it's candle power from here on in."

Mel took her phone from her pocket and checked it. "My phone's dead, too."

Kelsey looked around. "Something is draining our power."

Total darkness enveloped them.

A snap, and then a flicker of light appeared. "Got it."

Jo passed a candle to Kelsey and then lit two more. She stood taller and Kelsey handed Jo a thick short candle. Two wicks burned on the top of the fat cylinder of wax.

Flickering with each movement they made, the candles cast shadows on the stone walls.

Mel stopped. "Okay, this is it. Here it is. This is the room where Edward and I found the Ouija board. I'll go in first. Hold your candles up high, so I can see where I'm going."

Mel opened the door and screamed. Jumping back, she almost knocked her aunt down.

Kelsey shouted, "What's wrong?"

"Mel honey? What's wrong?" Her aunt grabbed her before she could fall.

Mel caught her breath. "Damn, I'm sorry. Something just ran over my foot." She shuddered. "I don't even want to think about what it was."

Kelsey mumbled. "Cripes. Get a grip, Mel. You scared me half to death."

Stepping inside the room, Kelsey looked around in the flickering light. "Oh my gosh. This isn't exactly the *Magic Kingdom*. Is it?"

"Doesn't even come close. There it is."

Mel crossed over to the corner where an upturned box held a Ouija board and its pointer.

Jo stared at the Ouija board and then at the largest wall. She scanned the room in the dim light. Placing both hands on the wall closest to the board, she patted the entire surface. Confused, she began palming the other inside walls, shaking her head.

"This isn't how he's entering. The walls aren't his portal."

Mel looked up from the floor. "What? One of them *must* be. How else is he manifesting from this room? It has to be this room. The smell is strongest here."

Jo shook her head. "Sorry dear, but none of these walls are his portal. They're not warm at all to the touch... In fact, they're cold and damp. Feel them."

Mel jumped up from the floor and placed her hand on the wall beside her. "You're right. Now what?"

"Is there anywhere else down here where he could hide?"

Mel shook her head. "This is it. It has to be here." Puzzled, she stared at her companions.

"This doesn't make any sense. Someone is using this room for calling McGregor, so the walls should be warm from all the energy it took for him to manifest."

Kelsey stood by the Ouija board and placed her candle close to the dirt floor. "Well someone was here. Look at the cigarette butts stubbed out on the floor. They look pretty fresh. Whoever it is, smokes before they summon McGregor to this plane. I can think of better places to have my fifteen-minute coffee break."

Mel bent over and took a pair of tweezers from her pocket along with a small self-sealing bag. "Hold your candle steady for me, Kelsey. I want to study these closer in better conditions. The light isn't great here."

Kelsey gave an un-lady like snort, as she lowered her candle closer to the ground. "You're kidding, right? A tomb has better light than this place."

Without warning, turbulent air swirled around them, seeming to come from nowhere.

Jo's candle sputtered. "Let's get out of here. I've had enough of this place for a while."

———

Gulping in fresh, salty air, they stood on the back deck that overlooked the harbor. Mel raised her face to the sun, breathing in deeply, as the warmth of the sun's rays began to thaw her chilled bones.

Kelsey raised her arms, sucking in deep gulps of untainted air.

"Well, that was a lot of fun."

Mel grinned at her. "Ya think? You, my dear cousin, need to get out a lot more."

She glanced over at her aunt, who leaned against the exterior wall with her arms wrapped around her chest.

"What's wrong, Aunt Jo?"

"I can't understand it. This is the first time I've ever run into a room without a portal, but with the residue of the specter still present. That just doesn't happen. I need to call Andrew to check our files." She rubbed her cold arms. "Then I'm going to take a hot bath."

She smiled at her girls. "I can't remember when I've been so cold." She chuckled. "Maybe it's my age."

Mel stomped back and forth. "I wouldn't worry about your age, Aunt Jo. My feet feel like two slabs of ice. A bath sounds like heaven."

Kelsey nodded. "I can't think of anything I'd rather do right now, either."

Mel took one last look around. "Then let's get out of here. We'll think of something. There's a logic to everything. This has gone on long enough. We're going to nail him."

16

M el knocked on Jo's door and waited for an answer.

Kelsey leaned in against the door as well. "Maybe she's sleeping. Knock harder."

"Or..." Mel grinned. "She could be talking to Doug."

She tilted her ear against the door. "I do hear a noise."

The door flew open with the girls almost falling through the opening.

Jo laughed at the look on their faces, shaking her head.

"Some things never change. Oh and for your information that was your Uncle Andrew on the phone. I'm not speaking to Doug until this evening. So, move it, my bunch of nosey brats. I'm starving. Let's eat."

Mel gave Kelsey a sheepish glance. "That will teach us."

A subdued, but grinning Kelsey and Mel, followed their chuckling aunt to the lobby.

———

A waiter placed teapots on the table beside them.

Jo pulled a file from her purse. "I've been going over everything that you sent us, Mel."

She passed her nieces a copy of her file. "Is there anything that you think you should add to what you've already sent along?"

Mel shook her head, reading her aunt's notes. "No, nothing and what I sent you is very vague. The big question is, why is McGregor back here? He rants and raves, searching for something that meant so much to him when he was alive that he's willing to enter this plane again – after he died."

Mel nodded. "And, when he's summoned, each time he's stronger and more determined that nothing or no one is going to get in his way. Our only reliable information is from Katie. She keeps saying that he's after gold. Presumably, Archie Ramey's gold that may or may not exist. And there is no record of Archie's stash anywhere in Annie's journal." She shrugged her shoulders.

Kelsey blew air from her lips. "Let's just get rid of this monster. The gold is the least of our problems. Our biggest concern at this moment is who's behind the summoning of this horrible specter?"

Mel nodded at Kelsey. "It was the dregs of humanity when it was alive, now its malevolent essence is beyond evil. It must be stopped."

Aunt Jo grinned. "Who ya gonna call? The Gordon Agency."

The girls both groaned good naturedly at their aunt's take on *Ghostbusters*.

Jo's phone vibrated on the table. Checking the screen, she smiled. "Good, it's your uncle. I've been expecting a call from him." She turned her back to her nieces.

"Hello Andrew, did you find out anything new?" Nodding, she listened. "Yes." Pausing she smiled at the girls. "I thought so. I knew we had that problem before. Thanks Andrew. I'll pass that along to the girls." She chuckled. "Of course, we'll be careful. We always are." She held her phone away from her ear and frowned at it.

Speaking into the phone again, she sternly said, "Andrew, stop laughing. That's very rude." She rolled her eyes at the girls. "Good night, my brother. Sleep tight." Then, waving the phone, she grinned.

"I knew I was right. Mel, years ago your mother came up against a similar case. The manifestation wasn't using the walls as his portal, but rather used an object."

Kelsey frowned. "An object?"

Mel slapped the table. "The Ouija board!"

Jo nodded. "That would be my guess. None of us touched it or we would have realized that it was probably warm. I wondered because the walls were cold and damp. It has to be entering this plane from somewhere or something else. That happens, but not very often."

Jo looked up toward the door. "Now, this could become very interesting."

Edward walked toward them smiling and stood by Mel. "Hello, Mel."

She groaned inwardly and put her best face on. "Hello Edward. We have great news. We're pretty sure we know how McGregor is coming through."

"That's great."

Kelsey put her cup down. "We still don't know who summons him, but it's a start."

Edward still stood there next to Mel. Jo took pity on the man and although she and Kelsey could have read his mind, they decided that blocking him was best in their current situation. Not that they didn't want to know what was on his mind, but they didn't want to interfere in Mel's love life. In spite of what she had heard from Mel about his deceit, Jo knew Mel was inordinately drawn to him.

"Sit down, Edward, and join us. We just ordered. Mel honey, scoot over so Edward has some room."

Mel glared at her aunt, but moved her chair over as Edward grabbed a chair from another table.

She took a sip of her tea and breathed him in. God, he smelled good.

Taking her notebook out of her bag, she leafed to her most recent notes.

"Edward, do I have your permission to call your office and check out some things?"

He smiled sadly. "Mel, you can do anything you want to. I informed L.A. that you were to be given cart blanche, so fill your boots."

He checked his watch. "I have a meeting with Josh and Dan and then I'd like to invite you ladies for dinner. It will be a late dinner, if that's okay with you?"

Mel started to shake her head, but Kelsey jumped in. "We'd love to, Edward. We'll be ready when you are."

Mel cleared her throat. I'm not sure if I'll be able to. I have a lot of research to do. We're so close, Edward. I can feel it. I want to finish this as soon as possible."

His wonderful strong hand covered hers. "Mel, you need to eat so why don't I pick you all up at seven and we'll go to the Shore Club."

Before Mel could protest, Kelsey jumped in again. "Oh... Mel told us about the place. That sounds great. We'll be here."

Edward left and Mel stared at them. "I don't know how to ask you this, but have you picked up anything from him about..."

Kelsey shook her head with compassion. "About his wife? No."

Aunt Jo, nearest to Mel, patted her hand. "Mel dear, Kelsey and I decided to block all of Edward's thoughts. We knew you'd want us to do that."

Mel sighed. "You're right, I do... At least the well-mannered side of me does, but the other side of me really wants to know."

"I can tell you one thing, Cuz. I don't have to read anyone's mind to know he's head over heels in love with you."

Aunt Jo nodded. "That's a fact dear and we know you feel the same way."

Tears pooled in Mel's eyes. "I really do, but he has a wife that he would never leave and I would never ask him to."

Standing up, she wiped her eyes. "I'm going back to my room to do some more research until dinner time." She glared good naturedly at her cousin. "Why don't you guys go and do some shopping? We can't do anything until I find what I'm looking for."

"Are you sure we can't help you, dear?"

"No, Aunt Jo, not with this. I really won't know until I start digging. It's just a hunch, maybe nothing will come from it. McGregor's getting worse every time he's summoned. We might not be able to handle him when he appears again."

Jo hugged Mel. "Good luck, dear. You're going to need it. And hurry. We're running out of time."

———

Mel stared at the computer, shocked at what she was reading. Alice, Edward's assistant, had done a thorough job finding the info she was looking for. Mel hesitated over the keys, but she had to know.

She sent Alice a question. "What's Mrs. White's first name?" The name came flying back: Catherine.

Mel sighed, wiping tears that ran down her face. *Well now, do I feel any better?* She snorted. "Not one bit."

She deleted the answer and clicked on a genealogy

website. Searching for almost two hours, Mel stopped and backtracked. Staring at the screen, she couldn't believe what she was reading.

A knock sounded on her door. Thinking it was Edward, tears began to well again. "Jeeze Mel, get a grip." She mumbled to herself as she opened the door.

Aunt Jo stood in the doorway, carrying a tray with a teapot, cups and sugar cookies – Mel's favorite.

"Oh, Aunt Jo, thanks."

Placing the tray on the corner of the desk, Jo sat down on the chair.

Mel sat on her bed and faced her.

"What's wrong, honey?"

Mel wiped another tear, running down her cheek. "I did something I said I wouldn't do. I found out the name of Edward's wife."

"What is it?"

"Catherine White."

Puzzled, Aunt Jo poured tea. "Catherine White. Why does that name sound so familiar?"

Mel shrugged. "I don't know. Dan said she did a lot of charity work before her accident."

Jo passed a cup to Mel. "Drink your tea dear and try not to work too hard." She walked to the door, opened it and turned. "Don't forget we're having dinner with Edward."

Mel rolled her eyes. "I know."

Outside Mel's door, Jo punched in a number on her phone.

"Andrew." She sighed. "Yes dear, we're fine. Stop fussing. Andrew, find out who Catherine White is. Yes, that's right, Catherine White." She paused and listened. "I'd say check in the L.A. area. Thank you dear. Goodbye for the moment."

———

Edward was his most charming at dinner. He kept them laughing as he told more stories about the rich and famous.

Kelsey wiped tears from her eyes. "Oh my gosh, stop. My stomach hurts. I'm so full and you're making me laugh."

Edward leaned over and caressed the back of Mel's neck with his hand. She closed her eyes, treasuring each touch, hoping the memory would last a lifetime.

When everyone had finished, he drove them back to the inn.

Jo smiled as he opened the door for her. "Edward, thank you so much for a wonderful evening."

Kelsey giggled. "That goes for me too. Goodnight."

They left her and Edward standing together in the soft darkness of the night.

Edward pulled her into his arms and kissed her.

"Mel."

She shook her head, silencing him. "Edward, please." Wrapping her arms around his neck, she returned his kiss, hoping it would never end.

But it did. And pulling out of his arms, she stood there. Wanting to say so much, but so afraid to hear the truth.

He took a strand of hair that had fallen forward and placed it behind her ear. "Goodnight, Mel. Pleasant dreams."

With the memory of his kiss still on her lips, Mel opened the door and walked to her desk to check the e-mails from Alice before she ran her bath. Later, sitting up straight in her chair, she reread the last message.

"Oh my God. You son of a bitch. Got ya."

She called Emma to gather everyone together.

17

Mel arrived at the house and greeted everyone in the parlor. Jo and Kelsey followed close behind her. They knew what to do.

Dan and Josh sat in chairs by the peacock window. Edward leaned against the mantle by the fireplace, speaking to the men. He looked up when Mel entered.

She smiled and sat down by the fireplace, facing most of them.

"Thanks so much for attending this meeting. She looked around. "Emma's not here?"

"Here I am." Emma entered the parlor, concern written on her face. "Is it safe to be here?"

Jo shook her head. "Not really, Emma. McGregor has been summoned so much that there's no controlling him anymore." She looked at Mel. "So, make this short and sweet, dear."

Kelsey nodded her head in agreement. The rest looked around nervously.

Dan swallowed hard. "Couldn't you find anywhere else, Mel?"

"Sorry Dan, it had to be here. It's the most private place I know."

Aunt Jo's phone rang. "Carry on dear. I'll be right back."

"Well, I'll get right to the point. McGregor might start again any minute. It's been quite a while since his last rampage. He's out of control because he can't find what he's looking for. So, next he's going to attack whoever summoned him. If you see anybody strange, keep them away. He'll kill. We know someone's been coming in through the kitchen door and going downstairs, summoning him with a Ouija board."

Dan wiped his palms on his knees. "Mel, this isn't safe."

"No, it isn't Dan. That's why I'm warning all of you. Edward, I think it's time to close the house. You have a specter on the rampage. I'm sorry I failed you, but—"

Banging of the kitchen door brought everyone to their feet.

Josh hollered, "Come on, let's go. Let's get the hell out of here."

Loud pounding on the walls echoed in the silence of the room.

Kelsey rubbed her hands over her arms. "Mel, it's getting so cold. We have to leave, now."

Mel sighed. "Okay, let's go." Kelsey moved to the arches, but as she turned, she bounced back, landing on the floor. "Oh my God. It won't let us leave."

The pounding became louder, surrounding them. Mel ran to the door, only to be pushed back by some invisible force. She turned and screamed, "Oh no, we're too late. He's here."

The noise and roaring became unbearable.

"Okay, listen. Stand very still. At this point, he's only searching for the one who summoned him. He wants revenge. She shouted above the banging. "Keep still for God's sake, if you value your life."

A piercing scream rent the air.

Mel held on to Edward. "He's coming. He's coming. Thank God he's not coming for us."

Everyone stood, nailed to the floor.

Josh sprang into action. "I've got to go. I've got to leave."

Mel pulled at him. "You can't."

A roar of frustration bounced off the walls. Edward made a move to protect Mel.

"Stay still, Edward. I don't want you injured," she told him.

Another blood-curdling scream filled the air.

Josh dropped to his knees, screaming. "Stop him. Stop him. He's going to kill me."

Mel bent down beside Josh, while pounding and screaming filled the air with rage. "Josh, we have to stay. He's only looking for the one that summoned him."

Josh screamed. "I did it. It was me. Make him go away."

Mel went to the foyer and shouted. "Stop!"

Everyone stared at the still-sobbing Josh, kneeling on the floor.

Jo and a strange man stood in the doorway with large hammers in both their hands.

Mel stood over Josh with her arms crossed. "Get up. It's over."

Shocked, Dan stared at his friend. "What? What are you saying, Mel?"

She turned and faced everybody. "I'm saying that Josh has been behind this from the very beginning. He's been calling McGregor, his great-grandfather, back from the dead."

Dan ran and pulled Josh up by his shirt, shaking him till his teeth rattled. "You lousy bastard. Why Josh? Why?" He threw Josh back on the floor.

Mel stood, staring down at the culprit. "Because, McGregor's son was convinced over and over by his father, during the weeks before he died, that Archie Ramey owed him and his family. That's all they'd heard, all their lives. That a treasure, hidden in Lunenburg, rightfully belonged to them."

Dan's face took on a look that Mel had never seen before. He grabbed Josh from the floor and started pounding him. "You bastard. You almost killed Lenny."

Edward and the man standing next to Jo, pulled Dan off a screaming Josh.

Whimpering in pain, Josh crawled to the corner, away from his attacker. Spitting blood from bleeding lips, he glared with hatred through eyes that were already swelling from Dan's beating.

"It's mine. It belongs to my family."

Edward walked to the corner and grabbed Josh, holding him upright against the wall.

"You've no hope in hell of ever getting your hands on something that doesn't belong to you."

Dan tried to hit him again, but Edward stopped him. "He's not worth it, Dan."

"What do we do with this worthless piece of shit, Edward?"

Edward shrugged. "We can't call the police. What do we say to them? He manifested a ghost that caused wide destruction and almost killed someone?"

Dan tried to punch Josh again. Edward blocked his swing. "Well, what do we do with this asshole then?"

Josh put his hands up, protecting his face, glaring at them.

Edward looked around. "I'd say good riddance to garbage."

He dragged a cursing Josh out through the foyer, past where Lenny had lay bleeding and flung open the front door wide. Picking him up, he pulled Josh's face close to his. "Get out of town, you bastard. You're never going to work in any aspect of the entertainment industry again. I'll make sure of that."

He shook Josh until his eyes rolled in his head. "You have thirty minutes... Now move it, you slimy piece of shit."

Josh flew out the door, moaning as his body hit the hard marble.

"You've got thirty minutes to get out of town or I'm sending Dan after you."

Josh crawled on hands and knees to an urn filled with roses. After pulling himself up, he staggered to his car. Edward watched him leave then returned to the others.

"Maybe we should get out of here. McGregor might appear."

Mel shook her head and smiled. "I made that up, Edward. Come, sit down."

She pointed to the man who sat next to Emma. This is Bruce, Emma's husband."

Bruce held up the hammer and grinned. "Most fun I've had with a hammer and a boom box in a long time."

Jo smiled. "You better start from the beginning, dear."

Mel sat in the chair that Josh had vacated. Edward leaned against the fireplace, watching her face intently.

"Well, last night after dinner, Alice sent me some info on the crews you usually use. I had a hunch."

Edward interrupted her. "Hunch?"

Mel nodded. "Hunch. And it paid off. I went to a genealogy web site and found that Josh's father was born in Nova Scotia. I dug further and discovered that he changed his name from McGregor to Wells, taking his stepfather's name."

"His father changed it?"

"He did and moved to New Mexico where Josh was born. His father was an alcoholic, just like his grandfather and great-grandfather before him. The hate for Archie Ramey and wanting his gold was passed through each generation, woven into the very fabric of their being, so by the time the story was passed to Josh, he became obsessed with finding what he believed was his birthright."

She looked over at her aunt. "Were you able to read him, Aunt Jo, before Edward threw him out?"

She shook her head. "No dear, I tried, but he had me completely blocked."

Mel continued. "When Josh found out a movie was being filmed where his great-grandfather died, he did everything he could until he wrangled a job working on this project."

"Alice did a thorough check for me, Edward. All the references that Josh gave your company were fake."

Dan shook his head. "But, he was so good at his job..."

Edward stared at Mel. "So now what?"

Mel smiled, placing her hands on her hips. "Now I'm going to do what you hired me to do."

18

"Okay guys, watch your step." Mel led the way down the rickety basement stairs, followed by Jo, Kelsey and Edward.

He carried a large, cardboard box. "It's not safe for you ladies down here. Mel, let me lead the way."

Kelsey turned and snorted. "You're just lucky we let you come with us. It is rare, Edward, that a civilian is included when we destroy a portal. It's very dangerous. Sometimes it can backfire on us."

"Backfire?"

"Yes, backfire. Sometimes when a portal is opened... before we destroy it, the spirit could retaliate and that's not fun."

They entered the room and stood inside the door staring at the malevolent instrument, innocently sitting on the upturned box, just feet from them.

Mel and Jo moved toward it. Jo held magnetized spikes in her hands. Mel held the hammer in front of her. Mel stepped forward and took a spike from Jo. "Here goes."

Placing the spike in the middle of the Ouija board, she

took the hammer and hit the head of the spike with all her strength. Then she stood back.

The Ouija board rattled. A scream ripped through the putrid air around them. She grabbed another spike from Jo.

"Run, he's trying to get out."

Nobody moved.

"I'm the boss, you know."

Jo smiled. "Yes dear, we know."

Mel pounded another spike through the pointer and board, cracking them from side to side.

Silence replaced the screaming.

She threw her arms up in the air. "We did it. He'll never be able to return to this plane. Good riddance."

Edward, still holding the box, came forward. "How can you be sure?"

"These spikes are magnetized. The magnetic field acts as a barrier. No spirit can cross a magnetic barrier. They just don't have enough energy of their own to do it."

Mel grinned at Edward. "These are the 'proton packs' that real ghostbusters use."

———

They stood by the fire pit, behind the Ramey mansion, watching the engulfing flames devour the last of the Ouija board that had been McGregor's portal.

Kelsey sighed. "Thank God, that's over. Now we can go home."

The ringing of Jo's phone pulled everyone's thoughts back to the present.

"Oh, excuse me. I've been waiting for this call from your uncle," Jo told them.

Then she spoke into the phone. "Good news Andrew. Mission accomplished."

She laughed and winked at the girls. "Of course, we were careful. I'll tell you all about it when we return." She paused then answered. "As soon as we can get a flight out."

She paused again, listening and nodding. "That's what I thought. Andrew, I don't think I tell you often enough how amazing you are. I knew I'd heard that name before." She frowned. "What do you mean, what do I want?" She grinned at the phone. "Goodbye, dear. See you soon."

She smiled at him. "Edward, you never said a word about your grandmother, Catherine White, being a famous medium on the West Coast."

Edward chuckled. "It's not something you talk about when you're playing ball with your friends. It's hard to get it in, Oh, by the way Mel, did I tell you my grandmother talks to the dead?"

Mel grabbed him and spun him around. "*Grandmother?* Catherine White, is your grandmother? Not your wife?"

"Wife? What do you mean?"

"Oh, Edward. I've been such a fool. When your grandmother fell in her wheelchair, Josh told me that it was your wife that—"

"Is that why you became so distant with me, lately?" He pulled her into his arms, as tears of joy ran down her cheeks.

She nodded. "I thought you were married."

Grinning, Edward leaned down and kissed her deeply.

"Not yet, Mel Gordon. But I plan to be married, very soon."

———

Early twilight covered the sky with a kaleidoscope of color.

Cascading pink roses, planted in white urns, played tag with the soft evening breezes growing on either side of the weeping angel.

The four of them sat on benches in front of a memorial that commemorated lasting love and profound sorrow.

Emma sat on a bench with her husband, Bruce. "Well, we're here, Mel. What's up?"

Mel smiled. "I have something I want to show you and I didn't want a lot of people to be around."

She walked over to the angel and read the writing at the scepter's feet.

"Weep angel, weep for me. All the wealth in the world cannot mend a heart torn asunder."

Emma sighed. "I always thought it so sad."

Mel bent down and pushed the rosebud above the verse.

A click echoed in the early dusk. The front of the plaque lowered stiffly to the ground.

Emma sprang up. "Mel, what are you doing? Don't damage it."

Tugging at a three-foot square box, Mel smiled up at Emma. "Relax Emma. I'm giving you something Archie put here for safe keeping. His gold."

"Gold?" Bruce looked at Emma. "You mean the story was true, Em?"

Mel grunted. "I need some help here."

Bruce and Edward pulled the box from the base and carried it over to a bench. Twisting the handle, Edward opened it.

Gold coins gleamed in the last of the sunset.

Shocked, Emma and Bruce stared at it, their jaws slack.

Bruce took Emma's arm. "Emma, say something." She shook her head in amazement. "Mel. I don't know what to say."

Mel smiled at her." Take it home, Emma. It belongs to you and your sister."

Mel and Edward sat on a bench after a stunned Emma and Bruce left with Archie Ramey's legacy.

Dusk was settling in. Two little boys giggling, ran hand in hand past them, fading by their small headstones.

Edward squeezed her hand and smiled. "They're adorable, aren't they?"

She nodded. "Yes, they really are."

He took her in his arms and kissed her, whispering, "Just imagine what our children are going to be able to do."

She laughed and kissed him back. "I can hardly wait. I hope at least one will be a ghostbuster."

Edward tilted his head back and roared, his wonderful laugh echoing in the stillness of the cemetery.

"Oh, my lovely, Mel. I can hardly wait to take you home to Grandmother."

EPILOGUE

Mel sat on a chair in front of the stairs at the Ramey Mansion. Sun filtered through the stained-glass windows. She closed her eyes and called out in her mind. *"Katie? Katie are you here?"*

Soft orbs of tiny lights gathered together and the transparent ghost of the little Irish lass appeared on the steps in front of her.

Mel smiled. *"Hello Katie."*

Katie nodded her head. *"Morning misses."*

"He's gone Katie. I promised you I'd chase him away and I did."

"Oh miss, don't be joken' me. Are you sure now?"

"I am and he's never coming back."

"Oh miss, you're makin' me so happy."

"Katie, it's time for you to go."

"For all of us, Miss?"

Mel nodded. *"For all of you."*

Two soft orbs of light moved down the staircase and hovered above Katie before landing on the step where she sat.

"It's been a long time coming. Do you see the light Katie?"

"Oh yes Miss. I do."

"Move toward the light and let it surround you."

"I see it, miss. I see it."

Mel watched as two beautiful transparent women appeared beside Katie on the stairs. Smiling at Mel, they took Katie's hands in theirs and slowly disappeared.

Mel smiled back at the fading specters. *"Safe journey, sweet Katie. Safe journey, Emma and Olive."*

She walked to the entrance and looked back at the staircase. Mel smiled as brilliant specks of dust, danced and swayed in the warm sunlight, under the weeping angel.

ACKNOWLEDGMENTS

When I put that final period on the last page of Weeping Angels I heaved a sigh of relief. The book was finally finished. Now I want to acknowledge with humble gratitude and overwhelming thanks to my mentors and friends who helped make Weeping Angels a book that I'm very proud of.

To Pat Thomas, my editor, a heartfelt thank you for your wise suggestions and amazing input.

A huge thank you to a dear friend and an incredible writer, Cathryn Fox, for your formatting and enduring patience.

To my dear friend, Brenda Conrad who has been on this writing journey with me from the very beginning, from designing my book covers to editing. Thank you, Brenda

ABOUT HEATHER

Playwright Heather D. Veinotte has written and directed more than 26 plays for radio and stage. As well as being a recognized playwright, she is the author of two novels, "The Mystery on Skull Island"-A young reader book and "Beyond the Mist", a paranormal set in the 1800's in and near the historic towns of Lunenburg and Mahone Bay. Heather's very proud of the fact that this novel was awarded Honorable Mention in the prestige Writers' Digest Competition of North America. She was born in Bridgewater, Nova Scotia, the eldest of three children. Her love of stories began at a very early age when she would sit by her grandfather on his porch swing and listened enthralled as he wove tales about the "olden days" in Lunenburg County. Heather discovered the joy of books at a very early age. Along with the reading came the overwhelming passion to write, which she has never lost. She married her soul mate Bruce and together they have a son, daughter and two grandsons. They live in West Northfield, a charming community on the South Shore of Nova Scotia.

ALSO BY HEATHER D. VEINOTTE

Lonely Angels

Beyond the Mist

Mystery on Skull Island